BECAUSE
I DON'T
KNOW
WHAT
YOU
MEAN
AND
WHAT
YOU
DON'T

BECAUSE I DON'T KNOW WHAT YOU MEAN AND WHAT YOU DON'T

stories

JOSIE LONG

CANONGATE

First published in Great Britain, the USA and Canada in 2023
by Canongate Books Ltd, 14 High Street, Edinburgh EH1 1TE

Distributed in the USA by Publishers Group West
and in Canada by Publishers Group Canada

canongate.co.uk

1

British Library Cataloguing-in-Publication Data
A catalogue record for this book is available on
request from the British Library

ISBN 978 1 83885 608 3

Typeset in Bembo by Palimpsest Book Production Ltd,
Falkirk, Stirlingshire

Printed and bound in Great Britain by Clays Ltd, Elcograf S.p.A.

For my two London girls

CONTENTS

A Good Day

'You really want to kill your dad?' Amber says.

'No!' God, I panic so quickly I can't breathe. 'My stepdad.'

'Right.'

We've stopped by a drain. The water is up to our waists and grey. I can't believe how relaxed they are about it. I have never done anything like this before and I am trying to be calm about how cold it is and whether or not the drain is a sewage drain. What other type of drain would it be? The river's got a concrete base. Is that even a proper river?

Molly passed me a note and it said did I want to go out

on Saturday with her and Amber. The legend that is Amber from her primary school, always referred to, always talked about. She lost her virginity to a boy from St Dunstan's in Year 7, and she had to hide under the bed and sneak out after his parents went to sleep. I know she can take her bra off without taking her shirt off. I know her mum left and her dad just lets her do whatever she wants. She's allowed to draw on her bedroom wall and Molly says it looks cool.

A wisp of white plastic comes out of the end of the drain into the water right by us, and I freak out and scream. Molly bends down, gets it and tries to get me to lick it. God, I really am pathetic sometimes, it's embarrassing. I just want them not to know what a weirdo I am. I just want to get through this before I fuck this up like I fuck up everything. Amber doesn't laugh and Molly just stops and says, 'Babe, are you okay?' To me!

We start walking again and it gets really narrow, then there is a tunnel that is so tiny it's like just a big pipe and we hold our breath through it. At the end we have to plop ourselves out of it into this little pool, where the bottom is just mud and stones, like a proper real river, and the sun comes out and it just looks and feels really nice. I put my head under the water, my whole clothes and body are soaked anyway. We start laughing because we're all wearing wellies, like well done, that kept us dry. It is so funny. 'This is so, like, good,' I say. I lie looking up with my head in the water and I feel like the whole thing is just chilling me out. In the sky there's a willow tree branch and a magpie on it. There's one little cloud and there's a plane but it's still quite quiet. Molly and Amber splash each other and then we climb out.

The sun is focused right on us and we take our jeans and wellies and socks off. The sun is shining just for us! I haven't shaved my legs for weeks, shit, I forgot, and I feel my heart pound. Please God, don't let them notice my gross, fat, hairy legs. I know I ask a lot but please. Our feet look like wrinkly old dead feet. Amber has painted purple toenails and Molly has dark blue. I don't have anything, obviously, I am not even allowed to buy it, which is so unfair when Sarah has pierced ears and Leah literally has a pierced eyebrow. But they're bitches anyway so what should I expect? Molly isn't even looking at me. 'Tell Amber what you did last week.' Like it's casual but it's not, it's like a test.

'Oh, really? I mean it wasn't really me. I just—'

'If it wasn't you, who was it then?'

'Okay, it was me but I'm not getting big-headed about it or anything. I just know what I can do.'

I honestly don't know how any of it happened.

'Basically the truth of it is that I can control these things and I've always known it.' That feels too big. 'Basically I mean, not that I can control that much, I'm not as powerful as I'd like, but I am practising.'

'Charlie was doing a Ouija board and then called up a spirit and told them to give us a sign and then a spider literally that second came onto the table.'

'Yeah,' I say, like Molly has just taken the steam out of it. 'Yeah, and I said it wasn't enough and the light literally exploded that second after. And then when Soraya and Sadia tried to get out of the door the handle was blocked, so we were all stuck in the dark. But then I just knew the door would work again, so I told her to try it and it did. The spirit unlocked it.'

'Her parents go to spiritual church. They literally speak to ghosts all the time.'

My dad just goes to normal church. I shouldn't have said it but I lose track of stuff because it's just little things that don't matter. Like saying my dad supports Man United. But I want him to. It's better than the hellhole that is my actual family.

'That is so cool,' Amber says.

Wow. I just keep picking at a scab on my leg because I can't look up.

'Yeah, I don't talk about it much because it's not right to break the contract between worlds.'

Again maybe that was too much. I feel it straight away in my cheeks, this embarrassment, like instant regret.

'But it's just a big part of my life. But I would say I'm more of a witch than a Christian . . .'

That's not true.

'And I can do you a tarot reading if you want. I brought the cards – they're in my bag.'

'I would really like that.'

And then even Molly is all like 'me too'. I can't actually believe this, I can't actually get over it. Then Molly says, 'She makes up spells too. Like she gave Lydia this bag full of different herbs and told her what to say and then Mark Swinton asked her out. She burned sage in the corridor outside our form room and then Miss Anderson literally didn't come to school for two weeks.'

Molly looks to see what Amber thinks. She is so eager it's actually a bit pathetic.

I realise that I'm properly shivering, like I can't control it at all. My teeth start chattering, we are all just laughing so hard about it, but I'm also like, please, can we go back to your house because we could actually be dying. You know when you laugh so much it hurts the back of your head? It's actually tiring.

We walk round through the woods behind the road, holding our jeans and socks, my feet getting rubbed raw in the wellies, and every step being squishy and gross on the liners. I can't believe I'm basically just in my pants. Outside! How are they both so relaxed about it? They look so good and their clothes just actually fit. Not like me, I look ugly and disgusting. I feel too big all of the time.

Amber's house is like all of the ones on Crofton estate. Red brick and white wood little boxes. It looks like Lydia's house and my dad and Jan's house except the front garden is overgrown and the windows look old and peeling. When we get in we hang our clothes up in her garden and she gets us towels that are crunchy. They smell. We sit on a picnic table in her back garden and the two of them rock it side to side. Amber smokes. She's allowed to do it at home, but her dad is out anyway.

'Can we do the reading inside?'

That's too timid . . .

'It would work better in a place that has your energy.'

I want to go in her room so much. I hate smoking. It's so gross but if they offer I'll have to do it. Leah makes me go out with her 'to the shop' and every time it's just so she can smoke without mum and Paul finding out. And she says I'm boring for not doing it, but she is boring.

Molly starts talking about my stepdad again. I wish I'd never told her anything. It's like she enjoys it.

'You know about botulism? If you get his dinner and just let it cool down, and then you heat it up again, but not much, and then do that maybe ten times, he'll die but there's no evidence.'

'Who's going to eat a manky old dinner and die?' Amber says and blows smoke in Molly's face, then she looks me right in the eyes and my face stings and I look right down.

'You need to get a bird to come into the house.'

We go up the stairs. The carpet has been taken off them and there are those spiky things on each step that used to hold it there. The wood looks like it's going to fall apart.

Amber's room is so cool. She decorated it herself and every part of it looks amazing. She has a Barbie wrapped in a chain and covered in nail varnish hanging from the light. She has a mirror but it's smashed and has hand prints on it. Nothing feels clean. She's written out lyrics from Nine Inch Nails on the walls. When I get a CD I spend that night making sure I know the lyrics to all of it. I know it's Nine Inch Nails and I know Molly doesn't because she only likes Take That. And Lydia said that at her sleepover Molly made everyone watch the live video and it was really cringey. I am honestly glad she didn't invite me in the end.

A Good Day

Amber has got a double bed. When we sit on it it's like a circle but it's actually like me and Amber sitting next to each other and our knees touching.

I keep the cards in my mum's old scarf, because I love how it smells and it's chiffon which is really valuable. I shuffle the cards how I always do them. I practise shuffling them at home and it honestly makes me feel really calm when mum and Paul are kicking off. Then I get Amber to cut them twice.

I don't know what I'm doing.

I lay them out for her. Eight cards, in a circle with one in the middle, face down.

Molly is such a bitch, she's like, 'This isn't how you do it,' but I've told her my mum could be Romani so I think I should know how to do it.

'Okay, turn over the first.'

It's Death. Molly shrieks and looks at me like she hates me, but she's frightened of me.

'Death isn't actually about death, it's about change. It's about ending things that aren't good for you, like maybe relationships from your past that don't serve you anymore or make you feel like you're stuck.'

Fuck you, Molly.

Sod it.

'But it also is about death.'

The rest are just wands and coins, and I don't even have the booklet on me so I just try to style it out.

'The seven of wands is a new man coming into your life. He will be blond, and he will be interested in works of science and nature.'

My heart is banging in my chest but it's pretty cool and I feel like by the end everyone is a bit like 'woah'.

Molly's mum shows up about seven, and she keeps going on and on at Amber about her dad and her sister. She talks to her like she's her mum as well. Molly looks mortified but her mum is really strict so she's just standing behind her like a lemon. In the end she comes in the house and goes into the kitchen, looking through all the cupboards.

Then she goes. Suddenly it's so quiet.

'Sorry, I should've gone already too, sorry, I didn't know it was time to go, sorry.'

'No, you don't have to, my dad isn't back for ages. Hang out.'

How is she so sure of everything?

We go back up to her room and sit in her bed, like under the sheet and this zebra print blanket, and she shows me some poems she's written in this cool journal. We haven't eaten dinner and it's eight now, and it's all I can think about, but I'm just trying to forget about it. I shouldn't be eating anyway. She's so smart, she just gets it. She shows me the scalpel she uses to cut her arms. I show her the scars I've got, but they're so pathetic, I don't even have the guts to do it.

'Does your dad drink?'

'No, he just gets stoned. Does your stepdad?'

'Yeah, he's such a cunt. He gets drunk and just does weird stuff.'

'What do you mean?'

'Just gross stuff. Like shouting and, you know, like worse stuff to me and my mum and my stepsister.'

'Yeah.'

'I hate my stepsister. Everything is shit.'

We should do spells and we should write each other letters and we should hang out all the time. I want to sleep over and just talk all night. We can do spells in the woods. We could sell them, we could start a business doing it, we could be famous witches.

'Honestly, I think there's something wrong with me, like psychologically wrong. I just worry so much about everything that I feel physically sick. It happens all the time, about anything and everything. I feel guilty about everything.'

I wait for her to tell me I'm a fucking weirdo. Amber's actually psychic. She says she knew what I was thinking, she just knew by looking at me. She's always had that skill, like when she was a kid she just knew what people were feeling, always. It's so cool.

It is so late, so suddenly. Mum will double lock the door soon when she goes to bed and I know I have to go home but I don't want to go.

Amber's dad gets in downstairs and he slams the door. She looks at me and laughs at me for being frightened. I just sit in her room and hide while I hear the music of them talking downstairs. I hate overhearing, it makes me feel sick. When she comes back she's holding a joint (!) from her dad (!) and she laughs at me again. She says she knows I don't want to smoke. She is actually psychic. But I try it and it sort of chills me out, but honestly for about half a minute I thought I was going to die and I had to sit on the toilet and I felt so sick, and there's no toilet roll in there.

On my bike home the air feels like it's waking me up, but I'm still giggly, I just feel so light. When I scrape the kerb it's like slow motion and I'm watching myself fly onto the grass verge. My arm is all grazed and I can't walk on my ankle but it's still a bit funny.

I get in, and I try to walk so slowly and so silently into my room but I know everyone can hear the turn of the handle, the floorboard, even my footsteps. We can hear each other breathe, who am I trying to kid? My mum comes in to find me, and she's been crying so I hug her. Paul is still at the pub, so we can chat for a bit. When she goes my T-shirt is wet in two little circles on my shoulder, and I try to take it off and then I notice that my arm is covered in blood and gravel.

Lying in bed I'm just thinking about how I feel really, like, I can't explain. Like finally someone gets me.

Mum wakes me up at six, just shouting my name. I'm supposed to be at my dad's for church later but it takes me ages to get out of bed and work out what's going on. Leah is on the sofa crying and she doesn't look up at me, she just kind of moans.

'Tell her she can fuck off looking at me too. Look down! Look away!'

'What have I done?!'

We drive in Mum's car to Farnborough Hospital and Mum doesn't even have money for the car park. They leave me in the front seat so we don't get a ticket and they are gone for so long. And when they get back I don't even dare say anything. Mum is ranting and raving because the receptionist took ages to say which ward Paul was even in. I'm shaking and trying to just breathe in and out slowly. I don't think I can breathe.

My dad picks me up and he doesn't even know what to say about it. It's the first time Mum and my dad have even been in the same room for ever, and it's so fake and weird. And then he's trying to get us to still go to church, and that's when I really start freaking out and crying and I don't even think I've cried in front of my dad since I left primary school. I can't stop crying. I can't go into a church now. God, I am so, so sorry.

I'm waiting outside the front door when Amber gets here and I know it's bad but I'm so happy when I see her. All she does is hug me really hard and say we don't have to speak. I follow her all the way into the woods. I don't take my eyes off her trainers. I don't want to catch anyone's eyes, I don't even want to see where we're going.

She does everything for me. She digs a hole, she fills it with sticks and leaves. We don't have sage, but she puts brambles in. She rips up my diary page by page and she puts my tarot cards on it. She puts everything I could find on it and some lists we made at her house too. She's got her dad's silver lighter that has a skeleton and an American flag on it and we burn it all together. She does everything and I'm too scared to watch. Afterwards we get in the stream and I look up at the sky and she has to tell me to stop saying sorry the whole time.

We Decided
to Leave London

Does anyone want an egg? I have a spare egg.

At 8 a.m., this is how it starts for the day.

Yummy! I would like to take it if it's still going.

Instant reply. Who would have taken the one egg in ten seconds?

Is the egg still available? If so will text my daughter to see if she wants it.

There was literally a message two seconds ago.

Ooops! 🙂 *Just seen you've already got it @foldymole!? Let me know if you change your mind and I'll text my daughter.*

I can pick up the egg at lunch time if ok? Thanks again 🙏 🍳

Is it possible to get it earlier? Sorry would rather just get rid of it.

Who the fuck is desperate to get rid of an egg?

We are all losing our minds.

Last month it was a distanced line dance in the middle of the road. I've never seen so much physical tension made manifest. I have never wanted more for lightning to come down and strike me. I tried to focus on cursing the cul-de-sac. Picture it deflating into a deep sinkhole.

Darren has his own opinions about it all, and of course he's very vocal to me, but it's easy for him. They don't expect the husbands to participate.

It's a funny little street. It's split down the middle. Half of it is a terrace of two-bed houses like ours and the other side is the flats. Three low blocks with courtyards in the middle (and we all know which one is the council one). All of it used to be a sawmill. We bought our house from the plans and when we went to the little office we had to sign something saying we wouldn't eat anything grown in the soil. 'That's an auspicious start!' Darren shouted as we were leaving. He had a kind of boldness then, as if he was always two pints down. People thought it was obnoxious, but for me it was thrilling. Now what used to be a public performance is just for me and the cats, and for comments under articles about football.

All the little houses are signed up to the group, except for the obvious pariahs. Namely, that enemy family who upped sticks to somewhere more comfortable at the start of this, and the woman whose adult son sits out on the pavement smoking weed and staring down people walking their dogs as if he owns the footpath. No community spirit. I don't know how many of the flats are in on it, but I know the talk is that some people think they are too good for it. There's even talk that one of the courtyards has its own splinter group.

I'm not having people judging me.

Aaagh sorry to timewaste, i think the egg's not going to work for me.

No worries, hon. @Elaine_Ennis_Ipad do you want the egg?

Not for me thnks but my daughter might?

Sorry to interrupt #eggchat but does anyone know a plumber? Would prefer a woman if poss?

I don't even think plumbers are allowed to go into people's houses.

I suppose actually they must be.

My daughter doesn't want the egg.

Great.

About two weeks in, I get a knock on the door. 'Wait! Wait! I've got to get back onto the road!' I try to open it. 'Wait, I said wait . . . okay . . . fine . . .' Linzi from number 13. Lives alone. Retired but early retired. Bored shitless as far as I can tell. She asks me how I am as a way to start a fifty-minute monologue. 'It's awful. Just awful, isn't it?' The questions all seem rhetorical. 'And I mean poor Neil at number 1, you know Neil? Well, I'm sure you'd recognise him. Well, you know he's a travel agent so he's lost all his work. Lost everything. I mean I didn't even know travel agents were still a thing, I just go to booking.com, much cheaper. So kudos to him in a way for getting this far at all. But, yes, it's awful. I feel most sorry for the frontline workers, don't you?'

She actually pauses. I didn't realise this one required a response.

'Yes, I support them,' I say.

'Oh, we all support them.' Okay, Linzi, who leaflets for the Tories and shops delivery drivers parking in the designated residents' parking spots for longer than she decides is necessary.

'So I won't keep you . . .' It's been forty-five minutes. 'The reason I've popped by is we've started a community WhatsApp group! We decided to start one over on the Facebook group! Do you have Facebook? Nobody seems to have you as a friend . . . Oh, you do. Right. Nobody seemed to be able to find you. Well, we wanted to invite you. Do you want to add my page? Linzi Morton Herbalist . . . Okay, great. No, don't add Linzi Morton Hypnotherapist – that's not me. Honestly, that woman seems to be a fraud from what I can gather. I'm always getting misplaced complaints sent to my page. It's been a nightmare and Facebook won't even remove them. Don't you think that's wrong?'

I start to answer that yes, I do think that's wrong, but I see it was not a question that needed me.

And there they all were. All day and all night. The good households of Robin Hood Grove.

Just been walking round and seen all the beautiful rainbows. Wow. Reminds me of the show Rainbow. Anyone remember that one?

Fifty-two messages. Pretty much everyone has joined in, so I try to think what to say to let everyone know that I am not an antisocial person. *Yes, I remember that one lol.*

We should play it on a big screen on the green for the kids one night!!!

What a great idea everyone agrees.

I think there's five kids in total in the whole street, and flat 12 on the ground floor of the council block has three of them. Tall quiet girls who practise dances on their front lawn, unsmiling. I've never been able to work out how many people live there. I chat with the grandma (or the mum?) sometimes. She grows tomatoes in her front garden and none of them seem to have suffered from eating them. Then there's always three or four grown men coming and going. Always the noise of a football match coming out of the front window. Either side have long been bought and sold with their newly painted, muted grey front doors, little round plastic hanging plants and white wooden blinds in their windows. And then stuck in the middle is their flat that is too alive for the rest of them.

The only other kids are toddlers, placed almost perfectly apart so that you can always hear one of them screaming. I like kids well enough. I do. I really do. But, Jesus Christ, give me the love of a cat over that any day.

I see the mums all the time. Tina is put together and glamorous and Maria looks dead, but they have something in common so they get to make friends. I see them pushing their prams round and round the close. I see them running together in the evenings. They are leaving their houses twice every single day and I don't tell anyone. But I see them, and if I do, it means that other people must do too.

I walk at midnight so nobody can watch me and nobody can huff and puff right next to me. Darren made a show of being worried, but I said, 'Who's coming for me? They'd be scraping the barrel wouldn't they?' and he laughed at the joke, which I didn't appreciate.

There's a little path that people used to use as a short cut to the station, and then if you turn off it onto a little wisp of a space between two fences, you get to the scruffy piece of land next to it. It's too generous to say that it's a wood, but it does something. I am amazed that it exists, left here not making money for anybody. It's never pitch-dark because it's not big enough or far enough from the road, but it doesn't feel lit up either. I sit on the same tree stump every time and pretend I am miles from anyone. I call it my office. I listen out for birds and little creatures but I mostly hear tree cracks and creaks and sirens in the distance. I don't know why I started and I don't know why I keep doing it. I try to think of the last time I was out like this at night, and it must have been thirty years ago when the woods were the best place we had to get drunk as teenagers. I grew up in the middle of nowhere and I hated it. I'm not a natural camper. I like an all-inclusive. I like a cruise.

When I get in I try not to wake Darren, but the walls are made of cardboard. Plasterboard. I made the mistake of putting up shelves when we moved in, I didn't know any better, and they fell off, bringing great chunks of wall with them. It scared the shit out of me. It was only later that I got angry. The first three years of living here were a gradual realisation that we had been conned. The drains didn't drain. Heavy rain flooded the road. Black mould started creeping round the place and wouldn't leave. A whole street where every single corner had been cut and every expense spared.

Just a quickie lol 💀 *not like that Sue, but does anyone else rent out their parking space? Was trying to work out how much I could get for it?*

We charge the tenants on our other flat extra for the parking. Ooh how much pls? 🙏

We just googled what parking in a nearby long stay car park would charge. I'll text you the link but it's a good return. Watch out though because tenants can be a nightmare (sorry renters on thread I'm sure you're lovely!)

I throw my phone onto the rug under my desk. 'Am I mad here, Darren?' I call through the tracing paper separating us. 'Am I mad here? They're bragging about being landlords and it's winding me up.'

There's such a long pause I wonder if he's fallen asleep again.

'Should be ashamed of themselves, love! Where's Chairman Mao when you need him?'

'He's long dead, love!'

'I know!'

'I know you know!'

'Do you?'

'Shut up, you silly git!'

At least I can rely on someone.

The night we moved in, we bought champagne and fish and chips because that's what everyone said to do, and we got so drunk, and Darren's main theme was that we would never again pay a penny to a landlord! It's like a running joke between us now whenever the service charge goes up.

The next week it's a day's chat about how the local mutual aid group was trying to make things 'too political'.

'Everything's political, love,' he shouts through the wall.

I go over to my office early and sit down in the near dark. I stopped bringing my phone because I would end up just sat there reading the same things I had been indoors. I started to feel so small and so stuck. Like how is my whole life walking around this cul-de-sac and hiding in this same spot? I imagine myself like a little dim bulb shining upwards. Like a sparkler tracing the same sad little shapes every single evening. At first I felt so on edge with nothing to do and nothing to hold, I wanted a cigarette for the first time in a decade. But it's like with each night I am prac-tising being still and being quiet. I saw a fox with a tail that looked half chewed off. He stopped and saw me too and stayed for such a long time trying to work me out. My heart was going like the clappers.

OK so not trying to shop anyone but I need to make it clear that the flat courtyards are not places where groups can be at the same time, sorry.

Yes we have been troubled by the noise in the evenings regard-less of the rules.

So glad someone has said something. It would be a shame if the police got involved.

Nobody names the flat they mean, but it is clear as day they mean number 12 because they're the only ones who've dared to have barbecues out there. They're usually still at it when I'm walking home. Three phone numbers I don't have saved leave the group and I whoop from the drama of it. I run into the bedroom which is Darren's office at the moment just to tell him. Even he gets carried away and goes to the window to see if there's any real-world fallout. Only crickets out there though.

I've been thinking of something we could do for the kiddies!

In she chimes like she isn't wading into World War Three. No replies, just three or four cowards typing and deleting.

Just something I seen on Pinterest if anyone fancies it. Linzi, you in?

It's a link to a 'fairy garden' via some site that keeps trying to make me sign up as a member.

Oh yes please! It would be a good place for us to go and do some reflection about this year? I can lead a silent session if people are interested?

I got to watch the blossom coming out, and now I get to watch it coming down with the wind like a snowfall. A snowstorm on a warm night and a few birds rustling in the trees above me. It's funny, I remember a book I used to read as a little girl, about two little sisters who made dens under a willow, and brought snacks and blankets and chairs there. The pictures of a china tea set with dainty little plates, full of plums and tiny biscuits topped with meringue. Iced midget gems. I remember because I sent my mum mad until she got them for me. Easier that than a sister. The biscuits didn't live up to it, of course. What does? I sweep the ground by the tree stump with a stick like I'm a child making a den. I smell the scruffy ground and look for beetles and creepy crawlies. I keep expecting to have someone ruin this – teenagers out to get off with each other or people out to get pissed – but nobody ever does.

Darren comes in while I'm on a call for work and starts trying to make me laugh, so I pass him my phone to see the photos of the fairy garden and he starts off himself. Out by the middle of the green Linzi has put up a sign that used to say 'Santa Stop Here' and repurposed some gnomes. Someone else has painted the pebbles from their drive and brought them over too. There's a cellophane pond and a china cart horse from someone's lounge.

After dinner and a couple of bottles of wine I drag Darren out of the house for the first time in days. Sitting in my little den, I had to get several assurances he wasn't going to take the piss before I let him cross the threshold. Sat out drinking in the soft rain and chatting together like we'd sneaked out of our parents' houses. We don't come home till three.

Linzi is at the door at half seven. At least she has time to get down the drive while I'm struggling to put on my dressing gown.

'Have you heard?'

I don't have time to ask what I haven't heard before the monologue starts up and it takes me a good minute to tune in.

'We just know they're meeting up there most nights. I mean anybody can see how many people are coming and going out of that flat, at all hours. With children there! Don't you think that puts them in danger?'

We stand in silence for a moment because I am too hungover to contribute. It doesn't get in her way.

'It clearly puts them in danger, but more importantly it puts us all in danger. Our health.' She whispers the last word like it would be offensive to someone else over-hearing. 'Whatever it is, I'm going to be saying people have to start taking their security more seriously. I know it's the lockdown, but apparently there's been a crime spike because they're all so bored, you see. They've got nothing to do.'

The guys at number 12 work in the Sainsbury's Local up the hill. I've seen them. The dad or the grandad doesn't wear the mask over his nose, but I don't say anything. They've not stopped working this whole time. Isn't the mum (or the grandma?) a nurse? I want to ask but I'm preemptively interrupted.

'And Simon's house backs on to the alleyway and he said he's seen them going out to that scrappy bit of waste-land every single night, to smoke drugs. He thinks, anyway. He thinks they're planning burglaries out there. The police have been called. That's going onto the WhatsApp, don't you worry. The police have been informed as to who the suspects are and they've been informed of their movements.'

I am as wide awake and sobered up as if I had fallen into a frozen lake and I am shivering like it too. Is she making hints to me? She can't be. I feel guilty of something but I don't know what it is. I can't work out what I feel. I just want to get back inside.

The door is shut, but I can still hear her cry out once she reaches the green.

I silently count her steps back here and I open the door just as she reaches it. She doesn't even bother to step away from me this time.

I'm in my fleecy dressing gown and bare feet, bent down examining the crime scene. Doing my best to look shocked and scandalised. She's cradling a headless gnome in her arms and she looks distraught. A ray of sunshine is coming straight out through the clouds just to light her. It must be the hangover, but I feel like I've been punched in the chest because only now can I see how lonely she is, how brittle and wound up. I remember now she told me she has grandkids, but I've never seen them round here, let alone now. And just like that I am weeping in the centre of the green, at the demolished fairy garden and the smashed wine bottle and the sad little Santa sign. I hold her tightly in my arms, even though we both know we aren't allowed and anyone could be watching us.

A Little Dirty Thing

We get there late because we woke up late. We get there late because that morning we had sex on your kitchen worktop. When we were due to leave I started it and you didn't care if you got there on time. My arms were shaking holding myself up. And then straight after pulling up my jeans, tying up my sweaty hair, putting a necklace on as if that would hide what we'd been doing, make me look like a proper grown-up. Smirking and grabbing your arse in your jeans as we get in your car.

The first time I met you, you talked such a good game.

At a festival. I never do pills but I did with you. I said, 'Is it just the pills, or do you think you need to say that to me, you think that's what you're supposed to say?' You said, 'I don't know, I'm just saying it. You could be my girlfriend and be with me.' I said, 'Stop saying that,' but it got me. 'You want everything before it's actually there,' I said. You said, 'What?' And then the next thing we were sat outside and you were all over me. And I walked back home with my jacket and my cardigan and my mac all tied round my waist in a line, still high.

We get there late and you don't even know which house it is. It's sunny and we stink. I put my hand in your back pocket and you walk so quickly I can't keep it there. By the side of a little maisonette, under a rose arch, along a little gravel path, it's all so beautifully kept and designed. I'm trying to keep up with you but you're striding in there. A long table outside, it's like a photoshoot for a supermarket magazine. Doing a feature on summer entertaining. They're sat down already. Boy girl boy girl. Husband wife husband wife. Two blonde babies in high chairs. Salads on the table like nothing I've ever made myself. Peaches and goat's cheese and shredded mint. Fried carrots with flower petals. For fuck's sake.

Everyone is so gracious at him. At us. We show up empty-handed. No, we weren't waiting, you've arrived at the perfect time, you've brought someone, no, that's lovely. Hello! Hi! Hello! All round the table. My top lip sticks to my teeth and I try to run my tongue over it without looking like I'm leering. Everyone is dressed in French navy.

The men have great muscular definition. I feel like they use beard oil. The women have thought to wear sunglasses and been thoughtful enough to put them on their heads while they talk to each other. I pull at my T-shirt. Of course it has a stain on it. We sit down and his hand is straight on my thigh. They are not older than me but I feel like I am fourteen.

Are you drinking? Oh God, I'm so hungover still. He pours me a drink. I guess I am. Why not? This weekend I haven't been myself. I don't drink. Last night we bought hot dogs on the street from an old guy with a stand, the smell of the burnt onions seducing us both. We sat on a bench on the bridge and got off with each other. We had an involved conversation I can't remember and I made you buy me a Magnum from the garage on the walk back. I don't drink and I don't eat crap. I think if you knew me, if this was in real life, you wouldn't like me. I don't even know if you like me now.

The woman in front of me looks like an actress. Her hair is so long that she can toss it from one shoulder to the other and run it through her hands. When are you due? I say. Two more weeks. Just two more weeks, she laughs, I can hardly believe it. She rests her right hand on her stomach in a satisfied way and rubs it. That's wonderful, congratulations. The woman next to her laughs too. I'm as fat as you and I have four months left. How prepared are you? Oh God, don't start, he's not assembled anything, it's all in boxes piled up. Her partner leans in. It's always partner, not boyfriend, just partner. There's such an easiness to all of them. They all love each other. He grins. She's slandering me! I made a dresser. A changing cabinet, she corrects him. Okay, whatever, I did that. My hero. They kiss and she smirks over.

The host comes out. A pink shirt, an apron. Side parting like a war pilot. He's got a butcher's block with three chickens on it. Stacked up. Crisp and brown and perfect. He chops them with a real professional knife and we pass them round. All very polite, laughing and holding and moving and sharing the heavy platter and how many pieces do I take and who takes breast and who takes leg and everyone's so relaxed. I try to relax my shoulders. He puts his hand on the small of my back and it feels wonderful.

How far along are you? I say to the woman next to me. Still tinier than me but heavily pregnant. Every woman here is further along than me. I try to make a joke. I say, if I was as pregnant as you, when people asked me that I would look down, shocked and say, 'Oh God! You think I might be pregnant? Is that what this is? Oh God! One minute!' and then rush off. She doesn't laugh but she smiles with a kind of compassion for me. I eat a piece of peach with a knife and fork. They are all bright, clean and glowing.

Just get on a plane and come here. That was the text, and it felt so romantic and I had nothing left to lose so I did it.

I try to join the male conversation. The type of thirty-eight-year-olds who run a techno label. The type of glasses that change men's whole faces. A kind of flat lack of being impressed by me. I'm too animated, and I'm trying too hard.

He's talking about football. I try to pretend to care. I look at the side of his face. A few days of stubble. Wrinkles that look like little rays of sunshine coming out of his eyes. Thin lines of white where his sunglasses have been all weekend. Yesterday morning we woke up in a tent on the coast and the first thing we did was go down on each other. You licked your finger after it had been inside me and I thought it was creepy and too much, but I tried not to think that. It had been so long. We went into the sea in the nude and I saw someone in the distance and I didn't care. I think of all that and I get a little rush off it. I try to sound cool and make jokes. I say to myself, this is anxiety you are feeling, don't worry, just listen to me and take some slow breaths and drink your drink.

He turns and looks me straight in the eyes and I beam at him. It's involuntary. What is going on? I said to him last night. What are you up to? And he kissed me and it felt like being pushed up against a wall. Well, what is it we are doing? he said, and I said I didn't know. What is it that anyone's doing? Last time I saw him we slept together twice. I'm in London and I have a hotel, he texted and I went there. And we slept together twice and slept next to each other and left at seven, and I watched him wheel away his little wheelie suitcase. And I texted him after, that was a nice night, and he texted back yes. And sometimes while my boyfriend was asleep I would think about him and try to make myself come without shaking the bed.

And last night in your bed you put your arms around me and you said, I can just make babies with you. I can quit my job and make babies with you, and I didn't say anything because I don't know what you mean and what you don't.

They pass round ice creams and I eat one. I don't eat ice creams. The pregnant women all laugh together, the men drink beers. And I don't drink beers and I don't laugh.

Forgetting

'Meanwhile, back in the real world . . .'

Dad's favourite phrase.

If you're stressing about school or, most importantly, what someone else's perceptions of your actions are, remember to always go back to the real world. That's a fantasy you've created and you can't get sucked in by it. Worry wastes time and time is our most precious resource.

Dad digests books through an app because that's the most efficient way, and it means that he is one of the best-read people I know. Every morning he gets up at five because that hour is the best of the day, and then he can read the key points of two or three books before he works out. I did try to get up with him, but after a while it was perfectly clear I was too distracting and it wasn't the right morning path for me.

Now, my own personal routine goes thusly: up at seven, vitamins, water, fifteen minutes of general fitness training, thirty-five minutes of practice tests, five minutes of going over the tests with Dad, shower, breakfast (protein, carbohydrate and one piece of fruit), brisk walk to school. I used to get a lift in, but now it is perfectly clear I'm wise enough to go on my own, and the exercise at the start of the day is good for general overall focus.

When I'm at Mum's at the weekend she's totally slapdash, and so I often miss my routines. Diet is an issue too. So, time and time again, on Sunday night Dad will have me lay out sweet wrappers she's given me and we can then analyse them and talk about what would be a better choice. She quite frankly doesn't have a clue about this stuff and it's down to her mindset.

At school a lot of the children are either unambitious or just very childish. They don't have an emotionally mature attitude, which I have. As a result I have to just rise above it. Because if I am able to focus properly, when I get to my new school I will find my people. Dad says it's just a better class of pupil and when I get there I will appreciate the difference.

I used to go to after-school club every day, but now it's just Fridays before Mum can get there. It was simply a dump, for what they charged. Plus Grandad is retired now and he's lonely, so we have to humour him.

Monday to Thursday I see him hovering at the school gate. He is very enthusiastic but he is also really silly. His favourite joke is 'Life is like an all-you-can-eat buffet. You can't take it with you!' It doesn't make sense.

When he first started picking me up he asked a lot about Dad, about Mum, about school, about everything. It's annoying, and I don't know what to say. Thankfully he seems to have learned that it is not an efficient use of his time.

Grandad is Mum's father and, well, that is very clear. He is undisciplined like her. He used to be a teacher but at a college where common sense wasn't on the syllabus! He dresses like Jeremy Corbyn and Dad said he's just glad I won't need picking up from my next school.

Sometimes Grandad takes us into town, and when we walk around he is like a tour guide. I have to admit he has a good sense of humour. 'Look up! Look up at that sign! Stop! Two steps back . . . now what is that? What do you think that could possibly be? Can you see the writing on the wall up there, it's mostly faded away?' And sometimes I want to say, 'Look, Grandad, it's just a silly old sign, it's of interest to no one.' But he always puts in so much enthusiasm around it that I will admit that I find myself quite transported by him. He likes telling his version of pirate and smuggler stories – Robin Hood stories. There are always heroes who steal from the rich and give to the poor. Sometimes they're about people from when he was young who he says were audacious.

Grandad was young in the 1960s and 1970s, which was a totally different time. If we went back to the 1970s, we would be in real trouble. It was before Thatcher came around. One of the great Britons behind Churchill, John Terry and, quite possibly, Isambard Kingdom Brunel. When Grandad was young, he says, there was more community. A byword for people who want other people to do their work for them. Grandad says it every five minutes: community, community, community. He should put it onto a sweatshirt. Although that would be so funny as I can't imagine him wearing a sweatshirt. He only wears shirts!

Today should have been just like any normal Thursday, but welcome to my life, where things do not always go quite as planned.

I was late coming out of school because I hadn't remembered to pick up my trombone and I had to walk all the way back to our form room to get it, and when I was there Miss Crook waylaid me so that she could ask me about home. Between her and Grandad I feel like it's the Spanish Inquisition! I said to her that I simply forgot my trombone and that I would forget my uniform if it wasn't already on. Dad likes to joke that I would forget my head if it wasn't bolted onto my neck. I am trying to ensure that I can commit our schedule to memory, but I do sometimes lose track of whose weekend it is. I practise the trombone on Thursdays as that is when Dad plays golf and won't be tortured by it. He says the club is as important as the course, so he always needs to network and have a libation or two. I can take it to Mum's on her weekends too, because she is the one who cares if I play it, so it's only fair that she should listen to it.

If I had been on time, I think none of the fuss would have happened at all, and I wish I had been, but I had to get the silly trombone. But because it was my fault and I was late, Grandad was waiting at the gates at exactly the time his crusty old friend walked past. By the time I finally got to meet him, they were deep in conversation. The kind of conversation Grandad and Mum love, where they whinge about the council, about the government, about the past. Grandad's friend looks smart enough. He is wearing a shirt which looks neatly ironed, but his hair is too long and he's wearing a cravat. He is the kind of person that would make Dad say, 'We have a rare sighting of a hippie in the wild,' when we are driving through town.

When he sees me Grandad looks really happy, and I feel almost like I can't cope with it so I look down at the playground and move the trombone to my other hand.

'Ricky!' he cheers at me. I am glad that I'm the last one out of school because my name is Richard. Like the kings except Richard the Third.

'Ted, this is my one and only grandson, apple of my eye, pride and joy! . . . Ricky, this is my friend Ted, back from way back when you were just a little smidge in your mum's eye!'

I offer to shake his hand but he bundles me into a hug. 'Your grandad's a legend round here, son,' he says.

'Oh yes, Dad says he's a legend in his own lunchtime,' I say. Frankly, I don't know what it means but it sounds impressive.

Ted raises his eyebrow and they laugh together. He says, 'Your dad sounds like a very wise man,' in a way that does not feel good and they laugh again. I feel sick for a second but if I just swallow I can come back to reality. By the time I can focus again Ted is walking off towards King's Park and Grandad is practically singing my name at me: 'Ricky! Enrique!' Grandad will not stop saying my name in Spanish until I say *si!* And it is frustrating but it is a bit silly.

Grandad says Ted is playing a gig at the club in town, and that just this once we should go. He has a cheeky glint in his eye when he says, 'Let's tell your dad we had a quiet evening doing homework at home!' I try to explain to him that if a venue serves alcohol then there is a pretty slim chance of them letting someone my age even through the main doors, but he is not concerned in the slightest. He takes my trombone and my school bag and he walks with a spring in his step that he exaggerates until I start to laugh about it.

'What shall we have for dinner?'

The weekdays are just clean eating days like any other, so ideally we should have grilled chicken and steamed vegetables, but where in town are we going to find a place that would do that? Town is a den of iniquity.

'I don't mean what you're supposed to have, I mean what would you like? It's my treat.'

I don't want to think about the question but I say, 'I think it's funny that people say it's my treat, when they mean they are going to treat you. It's not the person buying it's treat, it's a treat for the other person. They should say it's your treat from me, shouldn't they? Not, it's my treat.'

'That's a really good point, Ricky. Well, if it's my treat, then we're going to go and get burgers. And chips. And milkshakes!'

Grandad is a vegetarian, and I don't even think he drinks milkshakes, so it is quite funny that he would choose that, but I humour him.

After we have dinner, which I have to say was DELICIOUS, we walk all the way to the other side of town. It's funny because Grandad only wants to walk. I think it's so he gets to give me a mini-lecture. Dad says he can't get out the habit of it.

He tells me about a group of women called squatters from fifty years ago, how they just took hold of a building despite the rules. He tells me about how one time a group of men broke into the supermarket each night and gave the food away to people who needed it. He makes me repeat after him: 'Fences are a spell propping up an illusion: that the world around us is a prison, that the beauty which surrounds us is not a collective inheritance, that we have no right to live free and rich with the natural world.' He tells me too much. It sounds like nonsense.

'Every single street in this city has a real story behind it of a normal person, just like you, fighting back against cruelty, fighting back against deprivation, carving out something fun and magical for the community of this city. The stories of the bosses are boring, but they try to make sure they're the only stories you know.'

I want to say to him that the simple fact is that he has never listened to any podcast by a CEO, and if he did, he might learn something about how the world operates. I don't think Grandad understands that there are people who are building and not just protesting everything.

'The most successful thing the ruling classes have done is to make us all forget that there used to be people's newspapers, and unions, local libraries and community centres. Community! Do you know what that means?'

I don't want to tell him what it means so I just groan, 'Grandad! Please! Stop the lecture!' And he says sorry, he's having a senior moment, and we have a giggle about it.

Grandad knows the man on the door and he stamps my hand and winks at me. He jokes that I am a VIP. Grandad gets me a Coke, and when they pour it, it's a whole pint! I don't want to even count up how many teaspoons of sugar go into a pint of Coke. It's a lot.

'You've got eyes like saucers, Ricky,' he says and he laughs a lot.

The music is pretty raucous. It's a band of old fogeys and everyone seems to know the songs. At one point Grandad and a man I didn't even know lifted me up onto their shoulders to chant along to the song about coming out and fighting like men. Grandad even tried to convince them to let me play my trombone on the stage!

On the way home it is safe to say that we were both feeling very silly. Grandad said we were merry men. We were playing a game where you cannot, under any circumstances, laugh. Not even a little bit. But of course then it's impossible not to laugh when you have your grandad pretending to do parps in the direction of strangers walking down the street.

When we get home Dad is back early from the golf club, and I just know that I am going to be in trouble for something, but I don't know what. Grandad doesn't seem to notice and he says to Dad, 'James, James! You've got to play with us!' And I'm feeling nervous but excited because I do think that Dad would love this one.

'The aim of the game, Dad,' I say as confidently as I can, 'is that one person has to try and make the other one laugh, but the other one is not allowed to laugh under any circumstances.'

Dad does not look very happy, but I think he doesn't want Grandad to know it.

'So, would you like to play?'

'Sure. Fine.'

'Okay, Ricky, what does your dad find funny? What really makes him laugh?'

I try to think of times when Dad has been really laughing and I can't. And my mouth is dry and I feel a bit like I am panicking which doesn't help anyone.

'When he listens to his podcasts, that's so funny. And when he's talking to me about something silly I've done? For instance, if I've forgotten something, he says, "Oh, you idiot, you'd forget your head if it weren't screwed on."'

I try to laugh about it so that Grandad and Dad will laugh.

'Or he laughs at me when I fall over, or I can't do the lock on the seatbelt, or . . . like . . .'

'Like what, Ricky?'

'His name is Richard!' Dad shouts, and it is so sudden that I will admit I jumped and then I spilled my glass of water onto the table and Dad's laptop, and then that's why he lost his temper so badly.

Luckily I am mature enough to decide that it would be best to go upstairs and put myself to bed in my room. But I could hear them shouting at each other and I couldn't tune it out of my ears. Dad was so angry, and then Grandad sounded angry in a way I have not heard before.

I went to the top of the stairs to listen. I can walk totally silently across the landing because it is important that I don't disturb anyone with my clown feet. They were shouting about me.

'And what if he fails? What then? You just going to punish him and make him feel a failure? What's he supposed to do? He's a little boy for Christ's sake!'

And Dad is swearing and saying he doesn't want to bring up a loser like Grandad, and here comes his favourite: 'Meanwhile, back in the real world, some of us care about success!'

'Don't make me laugh, son. You've driven every business you've ever had into the ground. How you've kept this place is a miracle.'

'I'm building something better for me and him.'

'All you care about is money. The best you can possibly imagine is a boot on your face so you chose to lick it!'

Then Dad starts telling Grandad swear words and to leave, and, I can't help it, I run down the stairs and I am crying, even though it is very babyish of me. And I tell Dad to stop, stop it, leave him alone!

Grandad is at the front door and he bends down to hug me. He says quickly, in a quiet voice, 'Your father, he wants you to think the world is a certain way, but he is just one person. Okay? Everyone is different, and the world isn't one way or another. Okay?'

I know, Grandad. Life is what you make of it, and I intend to make a lot of my time, my skills and my resources.

After Dad shuts the door he is calm and he puts his arm around me. 'Richard, you see now how he can get like Mum, when she was so crazy? You can understand now that you're eleven why it is that it's you and me against the world.'

In my head a memory jumps out of Dad and Mum when I was two or three, in the living room, fighting, her calling at me to get upstairs, to run, to hide. Blood on her face. I had forgotten.

At the weekend at Mum's I tell her, 'Grandad is not a topic up for discussion and that is that.' But he tries calling on her landline and she hands it to me.

'Ricky, love, I want to say sorry. Just know that I love you no matter what. It doesn't change if you do well or do badly. It doesn't ever change.'

He makes me cry, and all I can say is: 'Why did you have to shout, Grandad? Why did you have to shout like him?'

Grandad's quotes are from a brilliant photo essay by Right to Roam activist Jonathan Moses from his Twitter: 'Fences are a spell propping up an illusion: that the world around us is a prison, that the beauty which surrounds us is not a collective inheritance, that we have no right to live free and rich with the natural world. We make the world in our minds before we live it and live the impoverished reality our mind has been trained to inhabit. The power of that spell diminishes with every transgression. Our daily trespasses are not to be forgiven but celebrated. The more you act as though the world is already free, the more it is.'

Gallus

The day I met you, you did some kind of magic to me.

What I remember is that before it you were just some friend of Tommy's who was sent to pick me up. I leant against the railings at the station to take a breath, and you looked at me, and it lasted less than a second, but in that less than a second I knew and you knew. And after that I was self-conscious and shy. You were a stranger and then you weren't anymore.

On the drive to the house we talked about your work and about my journey like we were pretending to have small talk. There were no streetlights after the station road, and suddenly it was dark all around us. In the day, you said, the journey was beautiful and you pointed out where I would see hills if I could see anything at all. The road was still and clear, and we drove for nearly an hour. Two stags crossed the road and we stopped to wait for them. The shock of seeing them, the shock of the sudden stop. They were so tall and staring right at us, totally unafraid and in no hurry. We watched them and didn't say a word until they left, and you slowly started the car up again.

'Welcome to Scotland!' you said, and winked at me. Those fucking eyes. The charm there.

And when we got to the party whatever it was had taken root and it wasted no time.

I ran in to see Tommy and hug him and tell him happy fucking birthday and I spent too long holding him because it had been too long.

'Michael look after you, eh?' Like a joke I wasn't getting.

'Yes, he was very kind to come and get me.'

'Oh yes. Very kind.' Like he was warning me.

I was busy finding a drink and I was busy finding Annie and Emma and trying to catch up, but my whole body was taken over. When I walked past you it felt like we were touching. When I sat on a sofa talking about nothing I could feel you looking at me.

'Because I think the thing I want to change is the medium and not the actual message of the work, like, you know, even like working in clay or something.' I couldn't hear a word she was saying because the heat of you looking at me was unbearable. 'I am still me, I'm still the one communicating these ideas — they aren't going to change because actually I'm the medium. If that makes sense? Does that sound really pretentious? Oh God, is that what you think? I know it sounds really pretentious, don't even . . .'

This feeling that I could sense you wherever you were, and that it was because you wanted me to. It was deafening and it was wonderful and it was totally unbearable. When I saw you out of the corner of my eye talking to other girls I felt sorry for them.

It was late too quickly. I was sitting on the steps outside the French windows with Tommy's little brother. In the big room behind us, music was on and people were dancing in a way that was really just a crowd jumping. Holding each other and jumping and messy red faces singing and shouting. I could feel the floorboards shaking underneath me. Tommy's little brother was serious and small, nothing like Tommy. He was telling me about a book he'd read on intuition, and we were both putting our hands on the stone between us, touching the little tufts of moss, and picking at them. I felt good for the cold air and his quiet voice. He asked me about Steven and I talked about us getting a dog.

And then I felt you standing behind us and I didn't even dare to look round.

'Alright, Andy?'

Tommy's little brother looked up and obediently moved over. You sat down between us without a word. All you did was look at me. Pure charm. Looking someone in the eyes and staying right there. Just to say, 'You and me. We get what's what. Not like these other jerks. You and me. Something's going to happen. Something has to happen. It's unavoidable. Meet me in the smoking area. Meet me round the back. Meet me in the disabled toilets. Brush past me. Touch my elbow as you pass. Stand with me in the hallway and we won't turn on the lights.'

I'm shivering as I follow you into the woods. I look back up at the party. Every light is on, so it looks like the house is glowing around the edges, sat on top of the lawn that sweeps down to us. Teeming with people who have no idea that I have left with you. We don't say very much. I don't even think I am very drunk. We are just taking a walk. We are just getting away from everyone. Nothing is happening and nothing is going to happen, I repeat to myself.

I can hear my breath and I can feel my heart shaking my collarbone. I feel like I can hear my blood in my neck. Soon we will stop walking, and you will turn round to me, and I don't know what.

You grab my forearm so that I don't slip as the path changes and starts to go steeply down. It's only a few steps, but my brain doesn't catch up to it, and we are past the line of trees and stepping down a small cliff. I feel so disorientated hearing the waves, seeing a full moon right above us, slipping down the sand and feeling the long grass scratch my legs. It's lit up and open, and now I'm fucking freezing. It gives us an excuse to touch. To find a little sheltered spot and look out at the curve of the bay, knowing that nobody else is anywhere near us. I don't know if I feel safe or unsafe – I just feel compelled, I feel ravenous.

When we arrive back the party's all moved on. For a long time walking up the hill the whole place is on show like a doll's house. Most people have gone to bed. Tom's brother is sat in the kitchen round the island with a couple of other earnest young men drinking whisky and nodding their heads. I see some girls I half recognise on the sofa, kind of asleep, kind of still drinking, kind of laughing together. Tommy comes out the back door with one of his friends from home who I recognise only that much. They spark up a joint, sit down and see us both, me now trailing behind when we had been walking together so close to one another I swear just a second ago. How has he gained so much ground on me that they're chatting and he's into the house, away into a room I can't see and I'm still walking up this lawn taking forever?

It's only when I finally get up there that I see how wasted they are. Tommy's eyes are all pupils and he's snorting and chewing as he's talking. It took me so long to realise when people were pilled up at parties. I would just think a friend was feeling loved up for us to see each other and how rare these times were getting. I took all of the love to be real and now it leaves me cold. I'm too squeamish and pent-up for all of it, really, even though I try to keep up and join in. I can't even really smoke, it makes me paranoid, it scares me, but I do it. It's like when I realised half the men at work were coked up. Suddenly I saw the whole company for the first time as it really was – scared little boys.

Tommy keeps repeating himself, holding his face too close to mine as he clings on to my shoulders, half to balance, half to keep me safe. 'Where did you go? We were looking for you.' And I say, just on a walk, Tommy, I wasn't gone long, and hope he doesn't notice how long it was. 'You're a special person, okay? I don't want to see you messing anything up, okay? Okay? Okay? Okay? Because I love you dearly.' —

I just want to get away because I don't know where he has gone and I feel restless with fear. I feel desperate to find him and not to let him out of my sight again, that if I don't hurry up and find him, he will slip away, or I don't know what. On the stairs I hear the melody of a conversation; it sounds fraught, urgent, but I can't hear the words. I stop still and sit with my cheek against the wall. It's nearly dawn. I think of when I was a kid. I could never sleep at night, and I would creep down the stairs, halfway down, and sit and listen to my parents. They didn't shout, they had quiet little hushed-up rows. I couldn't hear the words, only the tone that made me sick with anxiety. My mother's sing-song voice repeating my dad's name, needling for an answer that would not satisfy her.

They come out onto the landing above me, and she pushes past me on the stairs, a girl I remember he was speaking to earlier, that I was not threatened by one bit. I turn my head and see him stood at the top of the stairs, chewing the edge of his fist and staring in front of him with something like malice, or maybe nothing at all. He notices me and he smiles, and I practically jump out of my skin.

And I don't know how I end up asleep next to him on the sofa, but when I wake up I can see Annie is lying behind him and he is lying on her arm, and why does this feel like I've been winded and I can't breathe? So I close my eyes and try to pretend to sleep until we'll all wake up. Wide awake with my eyes shut and my heartbeat throbbing in my throat.

On the train back with a couple of boys from the party – boys I remember from St Andrews who studied maths or engineering or physics and wore zip-up fleeces all year round, safe nerdy hillwalking boys talking the whole journey so loudly because they are not on a comedown and not even hungover, I don't think – I pretend to sleep all the way to London. The whole time repeating his name over and over in my head, saying to myself how did you get under my skin, how did you get so far under my skin? Trying to pretend I am not getting closer and closer to home, trying to keep my life separate from the weekend I have just had. Trying to understand what has happened. I feel like a baby bird knocked out of a nest.

It's two months later when I see Emma again. I'm in Edinburgh, and she meets me in the New Town outside a café that feels perched on the hill at an angle that won't hold. The wind is too high to be outside, but it's sunny and she wants to make the most of it. It's not even 6 p.m.

but we order a meal. I'm not hungry, and I have ribs and a baked potato congealing in front of me. She's cut her hair into a thick red bob which curls forward under her ears. She's started wearing lipstick. She has a new job, a new flat, new flatmates – everything feels fresh about her.

When she turns her attention to me she looks concerned. 'So what happened with you and Steven? I thought you guys were . . .' I don't let her finish. We were. I can't explain it to her because I can't explain it to myself.

We talk for a long time about the dog.

She puts her hand on top of mine and squeezes it and holds it there. I am staring at the solid blobs of barbecue sauce beside it, and the smell makes me feel sick. Then, suddenly, like the wind has blown the idea into her head, she lights up with what she wanted to tell me.

'Oh my God, did you hear about the scandal from Tommy's party? Quelle Scandale!'

I try to make sure nothing about me changes at all, so I stay entirely still and unchanged, but my breathing is so loud all of a sudden. I look up at her, and she is smiling with satisfaction.

'So, Michael. You know, Tommy's friend? God, I wouldn't even call them friends, just cause he's Sara's ex and so he still gets to hang around, fuck knows. So he disappears off all night . . .'

I smirk because I can't figure this out. I want to tell her about it, how intense it was.

'. . . with Aisha, you know, one of wee Andy's friends, the painter? Did you meet her? And anyway nobody's any the wiser really, like we all had no idea on the Saturday because she's not told anyone. It's only on Sunday night when it's just a few of them having a few drinks that she's not acting right and Andy goes off with her, and she won't really say what's gone on except that she's seen him the next night with someone else. I mean fuck knows what he's said to her to get her to go off to the beach with him, and . . . God knows. But, fuck, right?'

She drags out the last two words so she sounds like an American. She loves to tell a story.

'Gossip! Don't get me wrong, it's a bit grim, I'm not saying he's done anything. Just how he's gone about it, then just dropped her like litter. And then. Fucking hell. So Annie's already gone by the Sunday night, and he's given her a lift, and she's said anyway that at the party they'd got off with each other on the Saturday. So he takes her home, he stays, yada, yada, yada . . .'

She pauses for dramatic effect because she thinks I am captivated.

'It's not until two weeks ago. Two. Weeks. Ago. That I speak to her and she's all flush because she's been seeing him all this time and she feels really loved up. And I don't want to say, you know, ahem, a-void! But then speaking to Tommy, he's like, how does he always do this?'

Two weeks ago I was on the train down from Glasgow feeling like my whole body smelt of him and his bed. I was reading and rereading his messages on my friend's sofa. Wide awake with the blue screen in front of my face.

And I can see him for what he is, and I can see myself

for what I am, but there is nothing I can do now to stop it. A superficial enchantment that has sent me mad. Walking back up to Waverley Station I see myself text him, and I see myself get onto the Glasgow train.

Now, when I remember it, I think, you did some kind of magic to me. I didn't realise till far later that it was a curse. But even that isn't true. You didn't do it. I did it to myself because I wanted to believe something magic could happen. So I gave that glamour to some hapless prick that I turned into a god and then a monster.

Poets Rise

I am woken up on my birthday by a chainsaw out my window. The management company is cutting down the willow tree. It is 6 a.m. and I've lost what I've decided would've been a beautiful hour of blissful dreams. I sit up in the bed and check my phone. I make a coffee on the hob, and when it is done I make myself birthday pancakes on the hob and try not to fall into the trap of being annoyed by the one hob. You get annoyed by the one hob, it starts you off and you get annoyed by the vinyl sink that drips water onto the floor. You get annoyed by the jet wash of boiling or freezing water. You get annoyed at the old strip-light flickering across the room and how it covers the middle and not either end. I'm saying once you start getting annoyed the whole day goes by and you're annoyed by the streetlight coming in through the blind. Ivy just said, buy a sleep mask, and laughed at me. I said I didn't have money to buy a sleep mask. Ivy said, sew yourself a sleep mask. I didn't have anything to say to that so I sewed myself a sleep mask.

They are cutting down every tree. I'm so angry. I glare at them. I start a conversation with one of the maintenance men. He says I will have received an email. They are doing it for security reasons. The landlord gets the emails. It feels like it is pinching me to watch them killing these big old trees. I am not a hippie but I want to sob. When I came to look round this place, I thought I would sit underneath them and read or something. When I came to look round, the trees were a big draw. It is okay, I say to myself: I don't really live here, I live somewhere else.

I go out the gates of Poets Rise and down the long alleyway between the industrial estate and the train tracks. We are next to the station, but they didn't build a route over. For twenty minutes I walk down, along, over the bridge and then back on myself and I watch the station the whole time. Why watch it if you are going to get annoyed? Ivy says. She says seek acceptance, radical accept-ance, accept it, allow it. If you go to watch the puffins on some island or some shit and there are other birds but not puffins, either you enjoy those birds or you go somewhere else, but there won't be puffins there just by you wanting puffins. I don't want to accept it. I want it not to be happening to me.

I live in one room. One room for everything. That's your kitchen, that's your dining room, that's your sitting room, that's your parlour, that's your study, that's your bedroom, that's your conservatory, that's your den, that's your lounge, that's your day room, and honestly I'm just thinking of these rooms to make myself laugh. That's your day room! One room to rule them all! One hob and black mould in every corner. A built-in cupboard that won't close. Your garden is a metal platform and a door, and it half opens over a railway line. No. I live somewhere else completely and I need the day-to-day to catch up. I sit and fantasise about buying a big bath. I don't know where you even shop for a big bath, but I dream of it – installing the fucker in a bathroom with an open window. Birds singing outside it. Jasmine outside it.

The train is ninety minutes, and I don't want to dwell on that fact today. My mum tells me about the things I could do with that time. I could be reading books about business and I could be learning a language. I am not doing that. I am sitting in my seat and switching my brain to stunned. I just want to eat a piece of tropical fruit in a way that is so passionate that it stops people getting too close to me. I'm lucky it's just one train, I'm unlucky it's from the whole west to the whole east, but I am lucky because I get a seat. There, Ivy, I am lucky and I am grateful. And I like my work well enough. We should be on contracts. It should pay more. We should get paid lunch breaks, but so many things should be the case, shouldn't they?

I like it because they let you use your imagination and that's rare. Jim is notionally the supervisor, but I can think of like two times he's intervened with anyone and there are twenty-five people here at any one time. Me and Ivy in one little nook, Mon–Sat, occasional overtime, and we do really laugh. And sometimes we share what we are doing and pool our ideas together. Sometimes we have to if it's connected anyway. And I like that if you think of something good enough here, then everyone starts doing it. If your ideas are good, they get to come alive and that feeling is rare and delicious.

I have the same clients most of the time. It's long-term. I have to start each day by checking in with them. Social media/texts/messages/DMs/inboxes. See where each of them is. That takes the first hour in itself. I like that too. I have ten clients, and three of them are legit funny people, two of them are just jokes but they don't know it. Three of my clients are linked with three of Ivy's, so it's work to talk them over with her. The daily tea.

Ivy remembered my birthday because she is a fucking great friend. Ivy got everyone to sing me happy birthday because she is a fucking monster. Ivy got me new head-phones with little ice cream cones on them, and a notebook and a pen that smells like American grape flavour. We eat our lunches together in the break room. A screen has moti-vational messages on it, and they transition in such a cringe way into one another. WELCOME TO THE REAL WORLD wraps up like a ball and bounces off the screen. A ROOF OVER YOUR HEAD ON THE SKY walks on screen upright like a cowboy, and turns on its side like it tripped up. I get it, it's a fun workplace!

In the afternoon Jim sends me a new client and that's a big deal. I haven't had a new referral for months. My birthday present from work! I look through all his information, and he does so many different types of things that I have him down as a poser to begin with. It's easy to get to know someone from socials if you haven't met them, but you need to properly go through it all. Go back as far as you can and keep notes. Keep the receipts, because anything is useful.

On the train home I am eating these little pieces of baked corn that look like teeth. Individual dirty teeth. They are so hard to crunch it feels dangerous to my real ones. Three posh teenagers opposite me are staring me down, so I start trying to be gross and sucking them loudly. They go back to chatting. Their summer holidays are coming up. I forgot about school holidays for a bit and now I want to go on summer holidays so much it angers me. When did I last have a week off? When I was in between jobs and I was freaking out. I overhear, 'Three weeks at the house I own in France,' and I reach my limit, so I put my earphones, that now smell like grape juice, in and listen to Sea Sounds Meditation 2. It doesn't work. I hear the announcements for every station and I smell a man's BO next to me.

The difference between me and those kids is luck, is all. So it's my bad luck, that's it. And Ivy would say, so turn your luck around. She has been saving since school. Just saving everything she makes. Everything she has is planned out.

I have two cards and a letter telling me I have moved into the next age category on my student loan repayment scheme so it's twice as much. The whole degree was on-fucking-line but they can send me paper letters.

In bed I keep thinking about my new client and what I can do for him. I think about going to another country and what it would be like. Eating grape jelly in America. I have to get a passport first. It's too expensive. Plus then I couldn't get a blue chip one. When Mum applied they turned her down cause of Gran. She couldn't even get a second-grade one, so I don't even know if I could. And then I would have to sort visas. I try to focus on a beach. I try to focus on a pine forest. It's too fuzzy, it stresses me out.

Jim says the key is to undermine, not destroy. We aren't here for stopping terrorists, we're here to nip things in the bud. So anything that unsettles or frustrates is perfect.

The standard stuff is easy. Once you get into their phone you can lock them out. Once you get into their emails you can delete receipts, cancel bookings etc. I am a curse that follows you: no password will ever not need a reset, no trip will go to plan. I will publish your drafts or delete your drafts, whichever infuriates you more. I will mangle whatever I can get my hands on and you will never quite trust yourself again. And if you tell anyone about it, they'll think you've lost your grip. Some people really do go off the rails, but then it's actually easier. They're less of a threat then, and all we have to do is monitor. There are already people who focus on writing on their forums, so it doesn't help us to overlap. Plus there's nothing funnier than as soon as they go full conspiracy believer, and lose their credibility, just for it all to go away again. They lose their life, then their mind, then their proof. But it's just traitors really, not anyone to worry about and not anyone to be scared of.

We are allowed to troll them, and that is a fun way to spend the afternoon. There's guidelines on how to time-waste, how to actually get people to think you're for real. I love it because it's like drama class, and I always liked the idea of doing a drama class. But also, honestly, these people are so naive. They engage. They take everything on face value. It's pathetic. They trust too much. Like old ladies leaving their doors open, but they're not even old. But at the same time they are like a cult. They don't ever open their minds. If you can't debate what you think, and then change your mind, you're a cultist. If you can't be persuaded out of your politics, it isn't politics. It's religion. They are so fucking embarrassing to me. They want to make out like they're the only people struggling. Some of us don't want to be victims. They do. So we can help them out with that.

This morning me and Ivy sat cosy in the meeting room and laughed at our clients' cringe night out. She thinks they're in love. She guessed way before they did. I say we should encourage it because I know that love makes you panic like crazy. It makes me remember Mum saying to me, 'You don't understand,' when she was crying about it. 'You'll understand when you're older what love's about.' I think about when I fell in love with Tom, and I felt sick to the pit of my stomach, and my whole mind spent all its time thinking of how he would leave me. I want them to be eaten up by that too. I want them to cry for three months when it inevitably doesn't work out for the best.

At lunch me and Ivy have a picnic in the corridor downstairs with the fairy lights. Ivy's reading the *Financial Times* on her phone, and I can feel her getting stressed out without even looking at her. Some scheme is closing, and it was one she had her eye on to get on. I don't know what to say to her. It's never this way around, so I try to channel her. 'This wasn't the whole plan, this was one little step on the way' is what I come up with. She breathes in sharply, closes her eyes and presses her long fingernails into the bridge of her nose. 'Yes.' Quietly, that's all she says.

I spend all afternoon on the new boy. He writes comic strips online. He works for a charity so he can boast to the world how good he is. He never deletes his photos. I draw a little sketch map of the flat he shares with his boyfriend. I map out his friends and acquaintances. I know a lot of them. I know the kitchen he volunteers at, because I raised their rent last year when I was working with the old head chef. He has this done-up cargo bike, and I spend twenty-five minutes looking back ten years into his Instagram just to see if it was a present. It wasn't. Annoying. I was hoping for posh parents. Posh parents are so helpful in shaming them.

He loves the bike. He fixes it. He photographs it. He photographs himself fixing it.

He named it. It's a girl! He loves her. I can't get over how much he loves this stupid bike. The tenderness in maintaining her. The pride in keeping her on the road.

I arrange over the phone to have the bike stolen.

I don't love phoning Max and I don't love that whole department. They enjoy their work, but too much, and I've heard stories they take it too far. I know for a fact that they put one of my clients in hospital during a raid that didn't work out. But they know what they're doing though, and it helps to speed things along. Plus, if you have something at your disposal, you should use it. That's what Ivy says. I agree, sure, but if you think I'm reading the books on entrepreneurship she lent me, you're high as a kite.

'Do you want priority access to it?' Max asks me the next day. Ha. It hadn't even occurred to me until then, and I'm shocked that, yes, I really do. I want to get the old girl for myself. Usually I can't afford this kind of thing, plus usually they have shit taste. It's not even that I like it that much, but I want it so desperately I just blurt it out: 'Definitely. Can you send me the link?' Max laughs at me, and I hate it, so I hang up. He doesn't send me the link until 5.55, out of what feels like spite, so when I go onto the listing I have to rush to get it before the end of the day, and practically run to the warehouse.

When I see it in the flesh I know why he loved her and I can't stop smiling when I'm wheeling it out. Little flashes of pride like, yeah, this is mine, to everyone. To the security guards who literally could not give a shit.

The first hurdle hits me once I've scanned out. I'm in the rain by the gates. I don't have a helmet, I don't know the last time I rode a bike that wasn't at a gym, and I am nineteen miles from my flat. The second hurdle is basically just reiterations of the first hurdle but put into practice. It takes me nearly four hours to get home. I get lost in Wembley. I buy and eat a chicken wrap, sat on a brick wall. My phone dies, and I have to use mini-maps on bus stops for the last hour. When I get to the building I have to carry the bike to the third floor and get it into the room. If I try and leave it anywhere else, the management company will remove it: there are signs everywhere. I wheedle it into the space between the bed and the kitchen, and pull the front door shut with my foot, through the frame. When I collapse onto the bed I am soaked with rain and sweat, and I feel elated. Maybe it's exhaustion, but it doesn't feel like it. My cheeks are warm and my hair is messy, and I'm still happy about it. The glow from the streetlamp is lighting me up through the blind. It feels like I'm in an advert for sports clothes.

At the weekend I watch reaction videos to old songs and look on the dating apps. On Sunday I go out on the bike around the country park. I can't get over myself. I even wish I could post pictures of it too. I carry her back up the stairs carefully. Mostly cause I don't want to damage her but also because the stairwell walls are made of what seems to be paper and the CCTV would mean the fine would know exactly who it should be sent to. I've just about shut the door when my buzzer goes. I recognise the voice but I can't let myself believe it – it's too weird – so I buzz him up.

And then, in the space of ninety seconds, he is outside my door. I lean over the bike to stare at him through the peephole. He's taller in real life, and he looks stronger and more confident. For a second I'm genuinely scared what he might do. Then he takes off his glasses and starts speaking in his creaky little voice, and I know this man couldn't hurt a fly. He's got a little speech prepared that he's launched into and I've already missed the introduction while I was trying to calm myself down.

'So I know this seems weird, but I thought if I could speak to you, then you might be able to see my point of view about this.' He waits. I don't even feel like I'm the one in control as I open the door. He almost jumps out of his skin when he sees the bike. It takes us three goes to get him in the door, and we can't help but laugh at the awkwardness of it. It's only once he's in that I realise I can't remember the last time someone else was in here with me. When he's installed, sat on the bed, I make him a coffee and then I make myself a coffee, and we can finally try and talk. But the whole time he's trying to explain how he tracked the bike down, I'm just thinking at a hundred miles an hour – it's like my brain can't cope. There's something really charismatic about him in person that doesn't come across online. He holds your gaze and he has caring eyes. His speech is so animated, like he's singing a song with it, and it's lovely. He smells nice. I know that's dumb but I sort of expected him to smell like old clothes or bonfires or something.

It feels like it's out of nowhere when he stands up, but I guess he was leading up to it. He bends down and removes a little tracker from under the saddle. Literally the same kind we use. I feel so embarrassed, like somehow I've been played.

'I know I seem insane to you, but bikes get stolen all the time, and I just didn't want to take the risk.' You don't seem insane, Stephen, you seem really wise. 'And I'm so sorry to even do this, but can I at least ask you what you paid, so that I can try and compensate you. I don't want to just take her . . . it . . . back,' he corrects himself.

I want to tell him that I know Maureen is a she and that he doesn't need to correct himself. I want to tell him all about how I know him and I want to tell him to throw his phone into the canal. And I want to tell him to get a passport and get the hell out of here, even though I know there's no way in hell they would give him one. Why do I want to cry?

'Nothing.' I'm embarrassed. 'I mean you don't need to pay me. It's yours, take it.'

He can't believe it, and I can tell he feels guilty not giving me any money for it, but I also know he has fuck-all money in his account. He will have had to borrow this from his boyfriend, and that's already a sore point for them now. I have to basically force him to take it, and his eyes well up. I help him out with it, and in the hall he says, 'Can I hug you?' And I shake my head because I think if I touch someone I won't want to let go. If I start crying, it won't ever stop. He takes it to be some kind of hippie consent thing and doesn't take offence. I watch him go down the corridor, and I watch him carry her down the stairs with love.

I want to run down to the front of the building and ask him to help me. I can't bear how much I want him to hug me, to be held by somebody else who I know is a good person. I hold it in and my chest aches. I open the back door and lean my head out to peer down. I watch him all the way down the alley. He goes fast, and he bends his head right down like the Tour de France. I know he's smiling and laughing in bliss.

I sit down on the bed and close my eyes, but I keep my bare feet out there, pressed into the metal grille of the balcony floor so I can feel the little squares imprint onto my feet. There's a breeze on my ankles. I open my phone. The code is wrong. I type it very deliberately. The code is wrong. I type it very deliberately. The code is wrong. I am locked out of my phone. I press it onto my face. I want to melt the glass with my forehead.

2021, 20/21

Of course, I knew they had moved here. People try not to bring him up to me, but my best friends are indiscreet. And of course that is fine: it was a very long time ago, and how can I say I haven't moved on? I am carrying the physical manifestations of moving on in a baby sling and on my shoulders. I am breastfeeding one and playing snap with the other. It was all a very long time ago. But still.

It's like when you think you see something in the corner of your eye, or that odd feeling of someone walking over your grave. I mostly don't think about them, but on some animal level I am aware that he is close and that I should protect myself. And sometimes I do a double take. But I had been lucky enough till now that we hadn't crossed paths. Especially considering how small this town is, how many people we both know. The friends who didn't take sides, despite everything.

Now I see her name on the nursery app, liking the little messages for the baby room. (His name. She took his name. He stole hers and ate it.) I knew they had a baby. Of course I did. She doesn't update her Instagram as often as I get overtaken by the urge and the weakness of checking it. The absolute adrenaline that tells me not to press too hard and not to like the photo, not to watch a story, to try not to make her aware of what we are all ignoring.

Today was the first time that we were both there at the pick-up. I like to think she didn't see me because I ran back across the road to avoid her. Just like I ran into traffic one time away from him. But I am noisy and chaotic – I looked and sounded like a chicken trying to fly. Any kind of cool I thought I had disappeared. I waited and I saw her leave, cooing to her little child serenely. I picked up Angharad and she screamed because I hadn't brought her any sweeties. She woke up her sister, who screamed because she needed to be fed, and we had a fifteen-minute walk. It rained. It was a relatively easy pick-up.

Today was the first time we were in the same playground. I felt her in our orbit but I ignored her as best I could. I made us leave before Angharad was ready, and she was furious at the injustice of it. And rightly so: she could feel that the reasoning was off. She's a smart cookie. I try to teach her to trust herself. That, and that she doesn't have to be dishonest to adults. For my sins. It mostly means parenting her is harder than it could be. And that countless aunts and uncles, grannies and grandpas think I'm some kind of monster because I let her refuse kisses and cuddles. They say, 'Give your granny a big kiss,' and she says, bright and breezy, 'No, thanks!' And they look at me like I am going to tell her off and I only smile at her.

Today was the first time we were at a birthday party together. I felt scruffy and too big. I felt dirty. I don't know when I last had time to shower. Hyper-aware of our mutual lack of acknowledgement. Then my daughter and her son were on the slide and it was game over. I caught myself staring at her from the side. Trying not to appraise her body and her looks. Trying to work out what she was saying with her clothes, her hair, her lipstick, the frames of her glasses. She is stylish. She's aloof with me, of course, but I think she's very warm with the other mums. I realise that I am trying to work out if she's a sexual person, if she seems passionate and soft. I am totally distracted. My thoughts are on repeat. 'Is she happy? Is she happy? Is she happy?' I try to believe it, but this panic and doubt just loops around. Is he the same as he was?

Well, I say to myself, it was a long time ago, and people grow and change. I know I have. I was nineteen, and back then I, obviously, thought that I could make no mistakes. If I could perform the life I want, that was as good as living it. I used to crowd surf at rock shows. I used to wear a huge fake fur coat. Swigging from a bottle of vodka, walking down the middle of the road, stomping over cars in my high-heeled boots.

I didn't enjoy any of it.

That wasn't the point. The point was to have done it, to have the story. And that was how I met him too, and he fitted in perfectly. Some kind of prewritten chat-up that was all swagger. When I kissed him he tasted of cigarettes and I hated the taste. And then I hated the taste for five years straight.

'Hi, I'm Jess,' I manage after the air is so thick between us that it is embarrassing.

'Hi.'

She knows that I know her name, but I feel like there's a script I should follow.

'You're Emily, aren't you? I used to know Jake.'

I used to know him, what a laugh.

'I know. It's nice to finally meet you.'

Something within her feels ice-cold, unreadable.

Then all at once her son is pulling my daughter off the slide and we are both at great pains to defuse the situation and to reassure the other mother that really it is fine. And Carys is crying, and I'm explaining that he is too little to know about turns, that he is only learning now about taking turns. That she is coming up for two and he is only just one, so he didn't mean to hurt her, and as I say it I stop myself. I nearly drop her off my lap. I pick her up and I walk away, and as I walk away I whisper urgently in her ear, 'He shouldn't have hurt you. Nobody should hurt you.

He shouldn't have hit you. We don't hit, we don't hurt. We take turns, we listen.'

We walk past their house at toddler pace on the way home and I am too distracted to function. I make us stop so I can peer into the living room. What is it like in there?

At the start I thought he was intense. And he was interested in a way I hadn't had anyone ever be. He would sit me down and tell me: 'I want to know every single thought you have, I want to know everything you are thinking.' And he was tall and good-looking. He told me he was a model. He told me so many times that he was a model. Or, to be precise, that he was scouted to be a model. And I could not believe that a model would ever be interested in someone like me. I was fat. I had been told I was fat, and that that was awful and ugly, since I was a toddler. My body was a problem that needed to be solved. Mum would prod my belly and say, 'We just need to get rid of this, and then we can get you a tummy tuck,' when we were changing for swimming lessons. I knew what the rules were. But then of course the second I started trying to relax again I would get fat again. When I met him I had taken up running for the first time in my life, and a boy whose degree was being funded by the army would shout me through circuit training in the park as a favour. I'm not sure what I was hoping for. I felt like something good was about to arrive, but it never showed up.

The summer I met him I had been dumped by the first boy I had loved. Joe Carter. The name on every notebook.

The one I calculated my love for in FLAMES. I had loved that boy so desperately that even at the start I could make myself cry just by imagining him losing interest. Once, he was late to meet me from school, and I convinced myself that it was his way of leaving me. I wandered round the park like Ophelia in the painting, picking daisies and crying.

I suppose I was a lot. But I tried to hide it from Joe, because I tried to hide everything from everyone. He had made the trip down from his uni to mine to tell me that he didn't want to spend his whole life having slept with only one person. (Me.) He didn't want to have only slept with me. He told me and I went down the corridor and threw up.

I cried every evening for three months. I drank so much that my body started storing the drink in my eyes. My chest hurt so much that I hugged myself to try and make it better. It ached, and I couldn't breathe. When I met Jacob it was the first week I had felt good again. Got dressed up, gone out to pull and to show myself off. I look back on that night like it was such bad fortune that the fish I caught was him.

Gareth and I do the washing and drying-up at our big Belfast sinks. Together in the golden hour when both kids are finally asleep, before Carys starts fussing and having to be put back down. She's not like her sister, who's out like a light. She has bad dreams and night terrors and she wakes when she hears as much as a whisper. We only get this little bit of time to ourselves before the work of the night starts up, and it's a nice time. We put house music on and we talk and joke and try to get the tidying out of the way as best we can before it all starts up again. The treadmill of chaos we call it.

This place used to be a chapel. We didn't convert it, but it's not been a house much longer than we have lived here. The living space is one giant room, the kitchen down one side looking out on the fields behind us. Once an hour three-carriage trains light up the bottom of the mountain in the distance. The rest of the time it is quiet and dark. The air, the birds, the space, the beautiful greens, the rains – how nice it is. We joke that it's sickening.

'How'd it go today?' he asks.

'Mostly fine.'

'And it wasn't odd, seeing her?'

For a week I had been agonising as to whether I should go. I had felt so nervous about her presence, the potential of an encounter, and then when it finally happened? It was nothing like I had prewritten it.

'She was fine. She's a bit of a slippery fish. It's not her really . . .'

'It's him.'

'Yeah, it's him. I honestly am never going to understand why he—'

'Why he came here.'

'Yes. Why did he have to? Why?'

'He has a lot of the same friends, I suppose? He was at Aber too? I mean he has as much right as anyone.'

'He doesn't.' I feel so instantly angry that I am shaking.

'Don't get me wrong. I'm not being funny – I know he was an arsehole – but it's been twenty years, like.'

I walk out of the room, glowing red and shaking. 'Yes, he has the same friends, doesn't he!' I mutter in a mocking voice. I have never trusted the group in the same way since.

I storm back in, angry, as if he's betrayed me too. 'It actually wasn't just that he was an arsehole, you know. It was worse. It was actually abuse.'

I say the last part so unexpectedly quietly. It feels like it's only been since he arrived that I found that name.

I mean, he was also an arsehole. He would say things like 'I wish I had something that I believed in as strongly as they do' when we talked about the Nazis, and his line was 'we don't need feminism because it's just human rights' when our friend James had made me cry in the pub playing devil's advocate. I would feel so anxious that I felt sick but I wouldn't know what to say back.

It was more than that. From the start it was all-consuming. I realised too late that my life was the thing being consumed. He would follow me everywhere, even to the toilet. He stayed one night, and then it was every night, and then it was that I was spending too much time on my uni work and not enough time with him. It was so disorientating. Like standing in the sea up to your knees and the pebbles shifting under your feet. Suddenly you aren't where you were, suddenly you're not upright.

The arguments would come out of nowhere, and I would lose track of how we had got to them. A riptide rushing in from every side at once, sweeping me out to sea.

What he said seemed to make no sense. Always angry about something small, or I would be in trouble for something I had not done on purpose. I kept dreaming of a referee, or an independent observer in a hi-vis jacket, just to turn to and give a look, like 'Is this right? This can't be right?' But instead it was him and his moods that could not be anticipated. Two weeks in, he screamed at me because I had made plans with my friends, tying me up in some kind of logical argument where the only thing I knew was that it made me feel queasy after. You didn't say that (I did), you didn't mean that (I did), round and round and round in circles.

I don't know where to start telling Gareth. I barely start, but he listens and he wants me to open up.

Later, after we have made up, when Gareth is fast asleep and Carys won't settle, I swoop her up in my arms and take her to the big room. She's sleepy enough to snuggle into my neck as I sit on an armchair. I pull out a crate of photos from under the sofa. I find the pack from back then and leaf through them. Like picking a scab I shouldn't. A little frisson of danger I can't explain the attraction to.

There he is. There we are. As we were. I study my face in every detail. Do I look sad? Am I hiding it? I look tired, I look blank, I'm posing. I don't find anywhere I'm laughing a big, full laugh.

A photo I took of him in his bed, staring straight down the lens. His old attic room. I can see why he intimidated me. We were nineteen, but he talked like he had lived. He had just broken up with a couple he had been together with. They were thirty. This to me was like a French film, untouchably sophisticated.

He had been to India. On sleeper trains. In a beach hut for months until he had to come home because he nearly died. While I had been wasting my time at sixth form, he had been living. I couldn't believe how cool he seemed, smoking little rolled-up cigarettes, with long trousers that the ground had frayed the ends off. He had incense and bidis and textiles from India in his room.

And while I'm staring at it I'm hit by how ridiculous it is. What was he doing in India that was so impressive? A stoned white teenager just bumming about. Getting in people's way and taking so much coke that his heart nearly gave up. The realisation was slow and deep – he was a loser. He was dirty and he didn't do anything. A model. Someone had given their card to him in the street. That was it. Was it a modelling agency, or was it a portrait scam from the shopping centre?

I'm half amazed that a thought, a way of looking at something, can just sit unchallenged, unexamined, for twenty years before you can take a look at it and realise that it's junk. Just plain wrong. Like the little lies our parents told us as kids, to make things more magic, or just for their own amusement. The ice cream van hasn't run out of ice cream and Jacob was a fucking loser.

Carys falls finally to sleep, and it's been a while since she slept on me, so I try to enjoy it. The sweet calming feeling of her gentle little presence. Her heartbeat like a rabbit's. Her snuffling like a hedgehog. Once, on a train, a woman told me my baby was 'some kind of elfin wood-land creature', and I haven't stopped thinking of her like it. I remember both times I found out that I was having girls that I was frightened. I didn't want them to have to live in a world so built to brutalise them. But each of them surprises me, and it makes me hope that they will somehow sneak through the fence of all this. Two little rabbits escaping the farm.

A few nights later I tell Gareth that I don't want to invite either of them to Carys's birthday, even though it's The Done Thing to invite the whole class. I agonise over how to do it, and eventually I send secret individual texts to avoid the dreaded nursery app. He tells me not to worry, it's fine. I invite everyone else. I invite our mutual friends. I try to swallow down the flashes of remembering who didn't take sides. How I tried to joke about his abuse because I didn't know how else to let them know. They didn't believe me when I hinted, so I just pushed it down and let them.

Only a couple of my best friends ever seemed to get it. Kate, who heard him call me ten months after I had managed to leave him. We had been walking around the Tesco Metro buying things for a barbecue. When we all still lived in London and spent our summers childfree and carefree on the common. He had rung because I had missed his birthday. Screaming and shouting at me, calling me a cunt and a whore. She told me afterwards that I looked terrified, then it was as if I just snapped out of it. It was because this wonderful voice came into my brain and told me I didn't have to put up with it anymore, or ever again. The voice told me to hang up the phone, and I did, and it felt so wonderful to be free of him! Free of him forever!

I am strong-arming Gareth into planning the party, despite the fact that I acknowledge it's OTT, and that she is turning two and would be happy with just a cardboard box. He is humouring me and I appreciate it. I'm washing and Gareth is drying, and it's almost nightly now that I remember some other shitty thing that Jacob did that I am boiling over to tell him.

'He was a chef, right.'

'Right?'

'Right, but he wouldn't cook for me. It was like he made us get takeaways. I wanted to eat vegetables but it was like he wanted to make me fatter?'

'Oh, right.'

'And he stopped me going running. Or . . . I don't know, I can't even explain it, it was just much harder for me to? Like, if I tried, there was always something else he needed me to do that moment. Or he would take the piss out of me trying. It was so little sometimes, I feel mad trying to explain, like I can't catch onto it.'

'He was controlling. It sounds like he—'

We are interrupted by Carys on the baby monitor. I should have sleep-trained her. I should have night-weaned her, but she's my last one, and I don't want all this to be done and dusted. Lying in the dark, breastfeeding her to sleep while I look blankly at Instagram on my phone doesn't quite live the romance of the experience.

I didn't think it would be Instagram that taught me how to talk about Jacob. At thirty-eight years old. My heart thumping in my chest while I lay there, trying not to wake her. It seemed to come out of nowhere. I was reading the stories of a sex expert I love to follow, who is so bold and so outrageous in what she talks about. She's so far removed from my life that it feels thrilling to read. And then she says, 'Ladies.' She always starts it, 'Ladies'!

'Ladies, you ever think about the men who said they liked you before and then suddenly you realised they actually hated you – when did you realise he hated you?'

A whole thread, a whole chain of women talking about men like Jacob. All these women. All these men. When I hadn't found anyone else in real life. There, plainly written: Sexually Coercive Relationships. It had been something all this time?

My heart is thumping and I tentatively unwrap each memory.

He made me feel that I was bad at sex.

Just little insinuations at first. Reminders that he had slept with a lot of women. That he had had better. That he had been out with a woman who was thirty and in an open relationship. These details terrified me back then, as much as they seem a bad joke now.

He made me feel like he would leave me if I didn't do what he said.

Sex wasn't about sex like I had had it before. Before had been fun, it had been close, and when it hadn't been about love, it had been with a friend, exploring things and talking all the way. With him it was about humiliation. He always seemed to want to hurt me. But somehow also so desperately boring.

Getting me to repeat things to him during it – 'yes, I'm

a little whore' – and I'm thinking, are sex workers as bored as I am right now? Because I am so bored and so angry. Even he never seemed to feel anything, never seemed joyful or exhilarated, just posing my body, going through some kind of script he never told me in advance.

Coming downstairs, blinking in the artificial light, I find myself saying to Gareth, continuing on from my solo conversation and not ours, 'He wouldn't stop when I wanted him to. That's . . . rape, isn't it?' I feel slimy and embarrassed, like I am almost joking saying it out loud when I never had before.

He wouldn't stop when I wanted him to.

He didn't treat my body kindly.

He wouldn't stop hurting me and spitting on me when I wanted him to. He only wanted to hurt me and I couldn't make it stop. Or I wouldn't make it stop. And so much more that I can't even remember clearly enough.

'And on our third date he took the condom off without telling me. And that is too, isn't it?'

I saw him do it, and I was too scared to say anything and I went to get the morning-after pill. Then I stayed for five whole years. I can't work out why, standing and looking from here and now. It was all so far back, and now I don't know. I lied to myself so much and so often that I don't know what the feelings or pheromones were now they are gone. I want to think there was a reason I stayed that was good and that I don't feel ashamed of. Some of it must have felt adventurous. Or that I could convince myself it was.

And I know I didn't have a good model for it. God, you don't know what it's like to have to walk through the broken glass in your sitting room and stop your mum from harming herself all the while she's saying, 'You don't know what love is. When you're older you'll understand.' Telling me love is suffering, love is compromise. Telling me to ignore the way he acts and the way that makes you feel. Telling me it's a lie when I say that I am not safe.

I tell myself that I am safe now, but even though I have my little family, every time we snap or our tempers fray I am back on high alert. Because the girls see how Gareth treats me, always. They are listening to us, always, and so they need to know that men treat women well. They will treat me how he treats me, and I'm paralysed with terror that we will fuck it up.

I look around the big room, littered and chaotic with toys, the living space, the dining table with its chairs made from the chapel pews. The big, warm kitchen with the windows steamed up. The tiny train passing by at the bottom of the mountain. It is a wonder I managed to get here at all.

I barely made it out. I think I was always going to leave, I knew I would one day need to, but it's still a wonder that I did. After I dropped out of uni I moved in with him, and I couldn't go back to Mum's and then I was trapped. It took me years to build myself up again because he had taken everything. Going to the weights gym on my own. Letting the hickies and cuts on my neck and my thighs heal.

And now he has moved here, for good, and I can't understand why. I try to convince myself that I am still safe but I feel like prey being stalked.

I see Emily the morning of the party, when Angharad and I are packing up the car at the big Asda out of town. I've gone bonkers spending money I don't have and the car is heaving. She walks sedately towards me, her little boy sat up in the empty trolley.

Is she okay? Is she happy with him? Because, honestly, I like her. I want her to be okay. But also, I think I finally would really like revenge. Or a reckoning. Or, I don't know, something! To shout it out so that everyone knows and stops treating him like just another dad at the playground. To brand his forehead, to make him pay penance. For some acknowledgement of what he did and that it did happen and that I haven't held it in for too long. Twenty years of not realising that I was allowed to object.

She half smiles as she walks past me trying and failing to shove a helium '2', a helium unicorn and a helium love heart into our little boot. All blown up, heaving and squeaking. In the end I tie them to the rear windshield and we drive home, laughing and squealing like we are the naughtiest mummy and big sister the town has ever seen. We laugh, and I wind the windows down so that we can laugh even louder.

The party in the garden is going as well as I had hoped. Little fruit kebabs and pin the tail on the donkey and lots of the nursery mums bringing present bags that we all know it's okay to reuse next time. Little bags of fruit-based fake sweeties. The floor is lava. It's good. Gareth is taking a lot of photos. It gives him something to do that he feels confident in. The older sisters are playing on the climbing frame. The weather is holding.

I am stunned to see her arrive with James and his wife. And then, a few steps behind, Jacob. Sorry, 'Jake'. A whole new man now, my mistake, Jake! He smiles at me. I don't know what to do. He knows he isn't invited, and they just don't say a word about it. It's a small place. They have the excuse of that.

At first I find myself acting out what a host would do. Taking the present, getting them drinks and food, going out of my way to make them comfortable. All it takes is a little smirk from him. A snake doesn't stop being a snake once its fangs are removed. And suddenly I'm quaking, I'm paralysed, I'm furious, I'm incoherent. I'm being rude and arrogant and shouting and sneering at him and at James and at her too. And she's just staring at me. Is she trying to tell me something?

Ever so calmly, jovially almost, Gareth takes Jacob by the arm and gets him to leave. I'm proud of him. Jake shows everyone what a good sport he is, how silly this all is, how crazy I am still. I chase them out and down the front drive, and I can't stop myself shouting, 'If you ever come near my fucking house or my kids again, I will kill you!' I scream it.

'Charming!' he says, unflappable, performing for the crowd.

After we clean up the party, Gareth and I wash up together. It's still light, and I watch my daughters running across the field behind our house. Keep running, little rabbits. I watch Angharad take a carrot to the donkey and feed him ever so carefully. A flat palm. Nobody will harm you. Nobody will touch a hair on your heads, or they will have me to answer to – a grown woman.

The Instagram quotes are from @Oloni, and the thread on coercive relationships was from @clementine_ford.

Bold and Brazen

Life's battered the boldness out of me, love. That's why it's down to you, the younger generation, to show them all what's what. And I'm glad you are, love. It's very punk. It's very post-punk even, which is miles better. Did I show you that record yet? Yes, of course you can look through them. Those guys? Part of a big movement in Leicester at the start of the '80s, all kinds of dance and hardcore, it was a hotbed. Not like now. No, of course they couldn't do it now. All squatted the scene was. And fanzines. Yeah, when I saw you'd photocopied that leaflet I felt my heart melt. I thought all that was dead and gone. You restored my faith in the world, but I've told you that a few times, you know I have. I saw you and my Miles, little shit so he is, don't tell him that, and your friend, that lad . . .? Aye, Cal, how's he? Yeah, yeah, yeah, sorry, they. That's all fine by me. I can call him 'they'! I don't mind all that, you can still teach an old dog new tricks. Not that it's new, is it? I mean Bowie was a they really, he just didn't know it at the time.

Prince! There's one!

No, it cheered my old heart! I saw you, all dyed hair and fuck-off attitude, and I thought you looked like that bird out of X-Ray Spex. Oh, you know them? Good for you, good work, well done, you. Aye, help yourself to the beers in the kitchen . . . sure, see you after, see you after.

What's all this chat? Don't mind me, I've just come to get Sue a G&T. No, Steven, you old wanker. Ignore my brother, he shouldn't be in here. He's the old lot, you see, he doesn't understand. What does Dylan say? Come on, Miles, you know this one – what does Dylan say? Oh, God love him, you'd think I didn't teach him anything . . . I am not drunk, Miles. Don't get on at me, you're embarrassing yourself, they want to know! In 'The Times They Are a-Changin''! Aye, of course I know it. I don't have to go online about it. I know these things.

I love your hair by the way, just gorgeous. Thank you, ladies and gentlemen, I bid you adieu. Sue? Sue? I've got it, sit down, keep your knickers on . . . or not! I'm joking,

Miles, you don't have to groan. Sex doesn't end when you hit twenty, you know. It gets better after fifty, if you want the truth. Oh, that's worse, is it?

I'll stay up a bit later. Don't be shy. I know what you're up to! You can smoke it in the garden, go down to the summer house. No, don't worry about the neighbours. Next door are tenants anyway, they're all out getting drunk half the time. I hear them. No, if I'm outside I do, if I'm down watering the roses I do. I heard them getting in late just the other week. Anyway, what does it matter about all this? Jeezo, go. Sue, can you imagine your dad letting us get stoned? It's a different world these days. Yes, exactly, you've got to embrace it. Facebook, all of it, I'm on it. It's the new rock and roll, isn't it? Minecraft. All of it. I'm going, I'm going. Come on, let's put on one of the oldies. Jesus, Sue, it's a different world.

What? No, I wasn't sleeping, I was listening. You should listen to her, Miles, she's got the right idea. What are you into then, Cherry, love? No, I want to hear what you've got to say. They should be listening to what you've got to say. I'm just resting my eyes.

Hop in!

You're up in the front with me, girl. You can navigate. No, I don't use the phone map. It robs you of what you do know. And what happens to the information? Where does it go? I don't want Elon Musk knowing every time I've been to Tesco's. No, I've got a paper one in the glove compartment with the CDs. Oh yes, I'm old-school in the car. Put whatever you want on, I've got it all . . . Tracy Chapman, Dire Straits. This your first time at WOMAD? No! I thought your mum would have taken you. Your mum not into world music? Shame, she looks like she would be.

Yes, that's the term, that's what the festival is. I think after thirty years I should know. What do you mean? Oh God, no, I'm saying nothing. Nothing.

Okay, one thing: is it or is it not the music of the world?

Right. Right. Okay. Fine. I stand corrected. Fine. We are going to the festival of the type of music we shan't name. What's wrong with you? I am not being sarcastic, Miles. I yield the floor. I yield the floor.

Right, so nobody here wants to hear the CD I made, is it? You are all ungrateful little fucks, ungrateful, ignorant, pathetic little fucks. Spoiled little shits getting everything done for them. I used to hitch. You ever done that? No, you're all too caught up in cotton wool.

Knock, knock, knock. Hello, campers. I am feeling a bit sheepish, yes, I am. I'm sorry I lost my cool a bit there. Miles will tell you it's the motorways stressing me out. Yes, that's exactly it, Miles – not everyone respects the rules of the road. No, Cal, it's fine. I just get a bit frayed but I've had a pee, and I've been into the Smith's and got you these. Dunkin' Donuts. No, right, Krispy Kreme is those ones, isn't it? And look in the bag – no, under the satsumas. Try a slug of that, it'll put hair on your chest that will, my girl. No, no, I wanted to check the seal wasn't broken, and it opened by accident, don't worry about that. There's a can of Coke if you want to make up some drinks for the rest of the drive. Let's get Bob Marley on. Your mum like that? You don't know. I'm sure she does. Why? No, Miles, not because of that, I'm not saying they all . . . that's not what I said. Yes, exactly, Cal, let's all stay calm. Just open the glove box and get Bob Marley out, love. Look lively. Great. We're jamming now!

No, no, I'm going to roll a joint and hold the fort. You kids have fun. I've got my paper and I've got my cider, and Jim's just sent me a text to say he's arrived on site too. No, he's retired, Miles. Retired. So he's not in the police, is he?

Don't mind me, I've got lots to . . . you're just talking to yourself now, John, come on. Let's get the Clash on.

Bum Bum bum bum . . . bum bum bummmm bum bum. I'm just singing! Keep walking. Prick.

You what, mate? Oh, haha, aye, Guns of Brixton. God bless Joe Strummer. Yeah, gone too soon. Yeah. Yeah. Yeah. Yeah, mate, you've got that absolutely spot on − he's better off out of this muddle. Can you imagine? Oh, absolutely, they've got all the good tunes up there. I always say it's him and Kurt Cobain jamming. Kurt Cobain? Nirvana. Yeah. Aye, nice to meet you too. I'm just going to be chilling with a spliff if you want to join. Oh, you're tied to your kids, are you? You have my deepest sympathies, sir. Good day to you.

Jim! Jim! Just little old me. The brats are all at some ghastly racket. Come here, you old sod. How are you? You're looking well. Oh, he's brought a camping chair, has he?

Lord Muck over here! I'm joking, Jim — pitch up! I'll get you on the cider. No, if it doesn't blind us both, we get a refund. Ahh. Good to see you. I've missed you.

What time do you all call this then? Was it any good, Miles? That's great! No, I've not been on my own, thank you very much. You've just missed Uncle Jim. He was asking after you. He's okay. Mary going has hit him hard, as you know. After the cancer. It's hard for us lot, you know. Oh God, no, I'm fine. I just get a wee bit sentimental at this stage of the night. Thank you, son. I'm fine. I don't get many hugs anymore off this one, Cherry.

Oh, doll, you've got a good little field kitchen there, haven't you? I'll take some beans if they're going, thanks, love. That's great. No, Cal, I've been on a little wander and got us some treats for the evening. Look at those . . . oh yes, they are that kind of brownies. How many other dads can get you those? Oh yes, they are that kind of mushrooms — yes, they bloody are! I'm not shouting! I'll take a coffee. Here's twenty quid, don't forget to tell your mum. She can see how tight I am, can't she? We'll hold the fort, won't we, Cherry? We'll hold the fort.

You made that skirt? Of course you fucking did. Wow. Give us a twirl.

Give us a twirl.

Come on, don't be shy, give us a twirl. I want to see if it flares out.

Oh, come on, girl.

I don't mean anything by it though. You've a lovely figure, proper curves, you can show it off. You shouldn't be shy about it. Come here.

The boys are back in town, are they! What you got? Coffees! Hair of the dog! It is when I put a shot in it, isn't it! Great, boys, great, boys. No, she's fine, just went into the tent to get changed, I think. She's not? You sure? I am asking if you're sure, Miles, you little smart arse.

No, we'll keep looking till we find her, Miles. She's . . . she's high! You never let a friend go off alone high. Oh my God, her mum will fucking kill me. She's difficult enough as it is. How did you just lose her? No, Cal, you're staying here too. I'm in parentis.

Gah! Fuck! Fuck!

We're just having a crisis, love, nothing for you to worry about. Keep walking.

Jesus Christ . . . old bitch, mind my French. Uptight old bitch.

Hokayyyyy, Cal, you're going to go to the lost and found, okay? You can do that? You feel okay to do that? Jesus Christ, boy, we are getting you a coffee and then you're going to the lost and found, and me and you will go up the direction she went off in, okay, Miley? Right.

No, no, Cherry, love, all's well that ends well. We were just worried about you. I'm glad you've slept it off. No, not yet, I was a bit wired. We've got the drive later, so I'm going to just catch a little snoozito in the tent then. I'm exhausted.

No, no, don't apologise now. I'm glad you've had an adventure. We should probably keep it to ourselves though, hen, haha. That's okay? Yes, but is it okay? Okay? Groovy.

My boy. Miles. Miles. Miles. Jesus, you're glued to that thing. Take the goddamned headphones off before I throw them out the window. Hello there, Cal! How can I hear him? Okay, *them* – fine, Jesus, *them*! I don't have to do it when he's not here. He can hear us through the monitor? What is this one? Which ones are you? Just pause the game then. Pause it. What do you mean you can't pause it? Don't shout at me! Who taught you to be so rude? He should respect his elders, Cal. Okay, fine, you finish and I'll wait.

So, I'm going to pick up Sue and . . . it's still not done? But it's all stopped, I can see it. No, you're not starting all over again. No. I said no.

I pay the bills, so, yes, I can turn whatever I want off, whenever I want. It's my house, mate. I'm off to pick up Sue – don't sulk – I'm going to pick up Sue from the station and I'm going to stop off at that place on the High Street and pick us up a pizza. See? Maybe you should have opened up those ears and LISTENED to me. What do you want? Oh, is she? No, no, that's great, you know that's not a problem. Why would it be? And the dough balls? Well, what does she eat? Of course she is. No, no, not a problem, I'll see if they do them. I don't mind! It's great, it's good. Is she good? Yes, I can ask her myself. Honestly, you are such a little smart arse, you really are.

★ ★ ★

I got them to make it for you specially. Oh, it's my pleasure, love. No, you don't have to thank me. Anyone would do it. How's your mum? A tribunal? God, good for her. No, they're all bastards, aren't they? Sue will tell you – she's been in the union for thirty years, haven't you? Aye. Yeah. That's it, Sue, isn't it? I'm glad to be out of it. It's harder for your generation now, I believe that. Yeah, Sue, nail on the head, Sue. But it's harder for us pensioners too. They change the rules. It's a pittance what we get. Okay, yeah, fine, but if it was my only money I would be really struggling.

You can have a glass of wine though, Cherry, hen. Come on, loosen up. Miles, have a beer!

No, fuck them all! Fuck them all! Burn it! Burn Westminster to the fucking ground! Why hasn't one single person taken a baseball bat to even one of them? Burn it! I'm sick of it! I want to see them with their heads smashed in! Oh, come on, Miles. Come on! Cherry agrees with me! Ha! You rebel! Cherry Guevara! Haha, you know who that is? On the posters? Cherry Guevara over here, Sue. Good for you, I knew we were on the same page.

Fine, Sue, let's watch our wee film then. I am calm. I am an ocean of calm. You know me, I just get passionate. Ask my ex-wife! It's a joke, Miles.

I'm happy to drop you off, Cherry love! Miles, I've only had two glasses of wine. No, she's fine with it. We can listen to my CDs! I don't want her catching the bus. I'm dropping Sue anyway. Sue, tell her it'll be fine. Exactly, Cherry – it's less hassle just to come along with us.

★　★　★

Oh aye, yes, I've been on every march going. You've nothing to worry about! They're a good laugh. I remember one of the criminal justice acts. You know about those? You don't? Oh, it was awful, honestly. They shut down people's freedom of assembly, stuff like that. Google it. I can send you the links. Or it might have been animals' rights. Those guys were a good laugh. Maybe it was an Iraq one? Anyway, one of those. There was a full samba band, and I managed to get in with them, walking along, shaking a rain stick and whatnot. So after, we'd all been fighting with police and I'm pretty knackered but happy enough. This was before Miles was born. Or maybe he was a baby. But he wasn't there. No, not safe for kids! So after, I end up at this squat. Oh, you'd have loved it, Cherry, this big warehouse where they practised and held parties and it . . . was . . . rancid! But the after-party was amazing. Get this, the police who turned up to shut it down ended up getting involved! They were pretty sound in the end. We can't judge one another, we can't judge one another! That's the point here, isn't it! We have to stay open-minded! And fight for everyone! Anyway, I'm keeping you waiting. We've been sat out here chatting away for half an hour! Safe home, give your mum a wee kiss for me! Hang on, before you go, I want you to take my number if you're going to go along on Saturday. No. No, lovie, nothing weird. I just think you need someone who understands looking out for you. Those things can get hairy, and if I can't be there myself, I'd like to know you're not getting into trouble. Miles will be at his mum's anyway. I can come and pick you up. I'll be back by the evening.

★　★　★

U lot ok down there? Haven't heard from u.

Ha gd2 hear it. Haha always weed on those marches lol. Send a photo pls.

Where's my photo ;(!

Did u get my last txt?

Steven, how do you get those pictures into a text? I see them all the time. Okay, walk me through. Oh! Would you look at that, a whole secret section!

[cat crying gif]

[vive la revolution gif]

[tumbleweed gif]

U all still up2 no good? I seen the kettle on the telly lol.

OK, GREAT TO HEAR YOURE SAFE AND TRY TO AVOID THE DREADED KETTLE [kettle sticker]

Oh my God, they've broken into the embassy? Bloody hell, Steven, they're dicing with death there. Those idiots! Is that live footage? Jesus Christ.

Are U ok?

Go4it.

Don't be frightened. Burn burn burn! Make an old man proud!! I will come pick u up if you need.

Put it on silent, Steve, if it won't stop ringing. I told you I am not answering it.

No, Miles, I don't know what you expect me to do. That was completely crazy what they did. No, Miles, I can't. Because it would put me and my whole business at risk. Because a police officer could have been KILLED, Miles. I said she was trouble the other week, after she was ranting and raving about revolution and bloody Che Guevara. Well, she's lucky it's just her arm, isn't she? That's the fucking end of it. Go to your room. No. Fuck off. Go to your mum's, I don't want you in the house tonight!

But that's the thing, Steven: they aren't realistic, are they? And they don't help themselves. They undermine their case. Exactly. They undermine it. Because if you're going to protest, do it like the suffragettes or MLK or Gandhi. Any of those. They didn't have to set things on fire, did they? You can't imagine Gandhi smashing up a McDonald's. We need something that unifies people, not something that puts people off. Even sympathetic people like you and me – we're on their side, but they're putting us off with this. What do they expect? It's all gone too far.

Three years, is it? Well, so be it. They got off lightly. As if they didn't think that would happen. It's lucky nobody was really hurt. It's the same as my tenants. Oh aye, grown adults and still living like students. The mess they left. The grout all rotten. They don't live in the real world. And always moaning about their debts. Moaning, whining, complaining. No, he's still at his mum's. Oh aye, exactly, tail between his legs. Little whelp.

Where's the real spirit in any of them?

Steven, how do I delete my texts?

Just an Informal Chat!

I arrive early, dressed how my sister showed me. I look right and I look normal. I'm the only person she knows with a tag and I know it embarrasses her, but she still wants to help because I'm family and she knows I don't have anyone else. I pretend I don't recognise anyone in the queue outside. I repeat my affirmations in my head, and when I am finally called I feel a little ghost of confidence inside me. Today is the day.

'We are really proud of the progress we can see that you're making in the home. I've been told it's tidier and looking more respectable now.'

'Yes.'

'And so we just wanted to have this informal little chat to see how you're getting on, really, if that's okay?'

I don't answer because I'm trying to unclench my jaw.

'If that's okay?'

How can her tone shift in such a minuscule way from cheery to threatening? Her smile hasn't altered and her eyes stay the same, but some micro-expression somewhere lets me know that I do not have the right not to reply.

'Of course!' I say, bright and breezy and smiling away. I got told once that actors have to deliberately think the thoughts of their character. They have to think 'I'm so in love with you!' in a love scene, so that their eyes do the right thing, for example, for the illusion to be fully realised. I think, 'I'm really feeling positive, so positive,' as I look her in the eyes. But I realise too late my mouth is pursed. The tension seeps out in whatever way it can. I'm not going to be a film star anytime soon.

'Well, shall we have a chat about your outlook on life now?'

She says this like it's nothing, just a bit of froth, and not absolutely everything.

'Of course. I would say I'm really feeling positive, so positive,' I blather without taking a breath.

'That's good to hear.'

She types something, several sentences' worth, and gives a quick, closed-lipped smile. The kind that people give on the street to say they are not a threat. The kind that has no warmth whatsoever.

'And have you been up to much?'

The question is as wide as the ocean. What is the right way to answer? I try to think fast and play it right.

'Yes. But only at home. I haven't been . . . causing any . . . mischief,' I try to joke. It lands so flat, so fast, that you'd think a gust of sleet had blown through the room. 'Sorry, I mean I'm trying to keep myself busy, but not get in anybody's way.'

'And how are you making money?'

'I'm trying however I can. I've been selling things online, and that's been clearing out my books.'

That feels like a masterstroke. Let her know I am getting rid of all those books they had flagged. No more mess and a normal home.

'And the added bonus of making some money too.' I add that and try to look pleased with myself, but not too pleased.

'I'm glad to hear it. Minimalise the clutter in your life. Entrepreneurial spirit, that's what we need.'

She looks pleased, but I don't know how pleased. I take a breath and look at the window behind her. The blind is sagging down on one side and the slats are in a triangle. Cars sit still in the car park, the grey asphalt and the grey sky above it.

Typing. For so long. She doesn't even bother to reassure me at this point. While still looking at the screen she says, 'And what about the elections last week? Did you go along and vote?'

A trap. I am no threat, I am planning nothing. I think this so hard that I worry my eyes look maniacally wide. 'No.'

'No?'

Fuck. No means you're not participating, which means you're criticising, which I realise too late. 'No, I did go, obviously, it's just none of them were for me.'

Digging further and further. Fuck, fuck, FUCK.

'So what did you do? You went along but you didn't vote?'

'No, I went. I'm just not explaining this very well. I went, but none of them were really for me, so I didn't remember that I went. I just went and took the paper, and I didn't actually pick one in the end.'

'A spoiled ballot?'

Even I can see how bad saying I had spoiled my ballot would be. Oh yes, I'm just going off to dig a tunnel under the bypass, and after this I'm going to lock onto an oil tanker again! I'm just going to live in a van now and see how you like my new lifestyle. Joking to myself doesn't make it easier. My mum used to say, 'You've got to laugh or you'd cry,' but you don't have to do either. I've found you can just sit, kind of catatonic, frozen in despair. You've got to sit and then further sit, that's what it should say. That amuses me.

'Oh no, I haven't ever done that.'

'I'm sure you have in the past?'

Can they know for sure? I shake my head. I hope they can't know for sure. They can't know for sure.

I shake my head again and smile. I think, 'What am I like?' I am a character in a comedy. If I can be a lighthearted character, she can see I am no threat and she will let my daughter come home to me.

She types, and then she turns her body to me and tents her fingers like a politician. She drops her smile and she becomes wholly a different person. 'With her father where he is . . .'

She doesn't even want to say the word 'prison'. It's distasteful to her.

'My problem here is trust. I want to trust that you have changed. But I don't. And I can't trust you to take on the job of teaching a child what the world is and what the world isn't when you don't accept it yourself.'

'I do know, I do know you can trust me. I'll say anything that you want, please, I'm begging you, I don't want to tell her anything or try to change anything, I just want to be with her. Please, please, please, please.'

I am crying. Thick hollow sobs.

I am still crying in the car park when I drop the tissue she gave me. I look around me and see the cameras and bend down to pick it up. I put it in my pocket and smile upwards. I pat my pocket twice. Don't worry, not a problem.

At home I write her a birthday card, scribbling fast like I am possessed. It says: I will never change. I do not accept their authority. I hate them. I will never change what I believe. I will never give up and I will never give up on you either. It says do whatever you can to destroy these bastards, do whatever you can to burn them to the ground. One day the spring will come and they can't stop it coming, my love, my darling. I love you.

I lick the envelope and it cuts my tongue. I press a drop

of blood into the seal. I rip it into shreds gently and slowly. I am very calm. I am a flat grey rock. I am an island unconquered.

Volunteering

'Did I already tell you about her? Oh God, I am LIVING for her, she is my LIFE,' she says to me before we have even sat down. 'Are we going to start with a cocktail? Let's start with a cocktail? Are you drinking? You must drink. Goody-goody.'

She orders us the special one for today, some kind of gin bramble with local berries. The table is too small and the chairs are repurposed from a school or a church: we both shift in our seats like that is all fine and good. It's the sort of place where the menu is written down the page in a series of cryptic clues. Ceps, Gruyère, Artichoke £19. It escalates. Chateaubriand, Mother Mary Greens, Chipped Maris, Red Marrow Rougère £87 (for two). I do not have the money for this.

'So her name is Sue. Which is perfect, isn't it? She's seventy-six and she's my BFF, my absolute old lady crush.'

I'm excited for tonight now. I've known Tara since we were fifteen and she is at her best when she has a new project. She was born to perform and she loves it. When she's fully immersed in a new obsession, it's all she wants to talk about, and it's like listening to a stand-up routine. Rather that than when the obsession is a boyfriend or a girlfriend. The woman is a magnet for drama. I used to think she was unlucky in love, but after a while I started to notice the common factor and then it was harder to summon any sympathy. Don't get me wrong: I care about her, but it doesn't seem to make a difference.

The way we work is that we meet up, she talks and I respond. I don't even know if she realises. I wait for the part where she'll ask her questions for the night – 'So how are you? How are things with Steven? How's work?' – all at once, so I have to pick one and shoot my shot. Usually afterwards she pauses, says nothing and goes back to her own concerns. She's done her duty as a friend, she's asked a question. And sometimes it drives me crazy, and other times I live for the gossip. What are you going to do? I'm not perfect.

To be fair to her, she doesn't think about me, but I don't think she talks shit about me either and that's comforting.

She knows a version of me that is harmless and uncomplicated. God knows who that person is. I feel angry and reassured that she doesn't know me.

'She runs that garden with an iron fist. And she knows everybody. Every single person on the estate.'

Tara loves to remind me she lives on an estate, as if she is no longer richer than me, or posher than me. Tara has lived on an estate for six months, since her mum bought her a flat on an estate. And I think her mum must pay the mortgage because she's left her job. Up until a couple of months ago she was working for an events company that put on charity fundraisers. It was run by a Hugo who she was at turns in love with, being hounded by, being ghosted by, back together with despite his wife, and eventually being fired by depending on the weather. She earned good money off the charities – nowhere near what he did, obviously – and, best of all, she got to say she worked helping people. Although the only people she really helped were the obnoxious drunks at the galas in banquet halls in the City.

Once she got me to waitress and I was stunned by the difference in her. She spoke in an even posher voice than usual. Nobody would have ever guessed where she went to school. She flirted with any man over fifty so wildly that I thought she was looking for a husband. To be fair to her, an older man would suit her to the ground. Someone who would spoil her rotten and switch off while she spoke at them. Someone she could cheat on and gossip about from a lounger by the pool at his country club. It would make good stories if I were still allowed to listen.

I entered a raffle and stole miniature bottles of gin that the guests were ignoring. I stole dozens. I ate leftover Beef Wellingtons in the kitchen with the other staff, and we laughed about the same rich drunk wankers. Tara didn't acknowledge me until every single guest had left. Then, in a cab back to mine, she told me about an 'outrageous, disgusting' guy who had tried to get her to go with him to the Seychelles. 'He must have been sixty years old,' she grimaced at me.

Her affair with Fraser lasted six months, and I had to hear about it for an hour a day. He never took her to the Seychelles, only to a grubby little flat he had in Whitechapel that his wife didn't know about. I think he even had tenants there at the same time; he just made them leave when he took her there. Gross.

Oh, and I actually won the raffle – £300 to spend at an upmarket pen shop in Canary Wharf. I tried to get them to give me the money but that they would not do. Going round thinking about how I couldn't pay my rent and what I could sell, and then going fuck it and getting a £250 pen engraved with song lyrics just to bump up the price.

'Volunteering in my community has changed my life. It really has. Like I have never felt such strong roots, I really haven't. Next week we have to do so much planting ahead of the summer. I think I'm going to be out most mornings and evenings just in the garden, and obviously some of the other volunteers don't pull their weight. There's this guy – I think he's in his late thirties and truly the saddest specimen I have ever met. Steven. I don't think he has a job. I don't think he's really got anything except the gardening. And he is so boring. Steven Smith – isn't that the most boring name you've ever heard? Sorry, I know your Steven is a Steven, but it is a boring name and at least he isn't Steven Smith. He just drones on and on. I literally have to pretend I need something from the shed and hide.'

This is where something familiar kicks in. She can't just enjoy this: it has to burden her and she has to identify an enemy. Just once I want for her to have something easy and pure. For it not to get gnarled up almost immediately and to become work for her.

'But, oh my goddess! I didn't tell you the best thing about Sue. So maybe three weeks ago when I first came to the garden meeting, she was giving us all an intro, mainly for me and soggy fucking Steven and a couple of hipsters who I actually think are teachers? Like when do they have time to do this? But anyway, she's giving us the intro to the garden, explaining it all, and someone says: so do we get to eat the vegetables? And Sue looks kind of mysterious, which I love for her. Then she smiles like a Cheshire cat and she goes: 'I don't.' Like, I'm sorry, but what? I mean what?'

I like this version of her. I like it so much better than when she found improv, and talked to everyone about how life was also improv, and kept discussing the details and rules of specific improv games to me until I felt like a coward for not shouting that I do not and will never give a fuck about improv. The past year she's done quite well as a sex-positive musical Instagrammer. She does shoots at the

GUM clinic and tries on underwear, and people send her sex toys for free. I think she does consultancy, I don't understand it, but she seems to be on corporate jobs with it. I think team building workshops where poor sods in offices have to tell her about how they masturbate.

It amuses me to think of her at sixteen, the most uptight girl of all of us. One Friday night sleepover, going round in a circle, each confessing that we did in fact masturbate, until it stopped with Tara pleading, 'Honestly though, I never have, honestly, if I had, I would tell you, honestly though, honestly.' The next morning she punished us all in her own way, kicking us out of her mum's house at seven, saying we had to be gone before she got up. She wouldn't stand being humiliated, even unintentionally. Especially not by us.

She moved schools the year of GCSEs, this glamorous arrival suddenly sat in the form room. Rumours used to fly about her. That she was an exchange student, that she was undercover police, that she was a ringer hired by the school to bring our grades up, that she got expelled for heroin dealing, coke dealing, arms dealing, everything. I didn't find out the truth for three years. For all her talking, she didn't want anyone to know that her dad was in prison and that she'd had to leave her private school because they didn't want the scandal. I don't know how they still had money, and I didn't want to ask. She was ashamed about it and made me promise not to tell. I didn't tell a soul.

'So I do have a theory. But it's kind of wild. Want to hear it? So Sue won't touch the vegetables, right? She's growing all these vegetables every year, and fruit too, and she has to pick them and sort them, all of that, but she won't eat them.'

'Does she eat vegetables at all?' I get to ask. She likes questions that further the story.

'Well, that's the funny thing, because she definitely has them in her flat. I've been in for a cup of tea. I know, I know, it was the greatest experience of my life – and I've had a threesome in a private plane.'

That's true. She told me all about it. I don't think she enjoyed it, and the guy whose plane it was left her in Monaco.

'Wait, let me just tell you about her house because it is such vintage Sue. You're thinking it's going to be all retro and old-fashioned, but I swear the flat is blinged out. Silver striped wallpaper, glitter on everything, you name it. A big mirror with neon writing in it that says YOLO. God bless her! She says she got it redecorated when she became a widow. Anyway, when she's making the tea I saw in her fridge and she's got vegetables, but they're all from the Tesco down the road.'

She takes a long, theatrical pause and smirks at me. 'So, obviously, that sent up a red flag for me.'

I don't understand, and our small plates arrive. Goat's curd and miniature herbs. A single courgette flower swimming in oil and chilli honey. A basket of bread that up until last year Tara wouldn't have touched, but now that she's sex-positive she's bread-positive too. It makes things easier. There was a time when she would insist we went out for dinner but then would only eat plain meat and undressed salad leaves, no matter where we went. I can recall her mouthing out 'undressed salad leaves' too slowly and feel how embarrassed I used to be, watching the waiters walking away smirking.

'I don't understand,' I say.

'Oh, babe, it's so obvious. So her husband is dead. She comes into money. She redecorates her whole place. She's finally free of him. Oh, and I should say I saw a photo of him in her hall, when he was younger. He was some kind of skinhead or something – okay, so maybe he was just bald but he looked mean as hell. A proper East End gangster. And now we know she won't eat the vegetables?'

She stabs a piece of yellow tomato with her fork.

'She killed him. He's under that vegetable patch! Think about it. So when they built the new block, this is five years ago, they wanted to knock down a bunch of stuff. A community hall, a couple of random buildings where they had meetings or, God knows, bike sheds, that kind of thing, and they wanted to use the allotments too, but she went absolutely ballistic. Sue was like: no way, no how, not on my watch! I mean, seriously, Sue was a community warrior. She got everyone on the estate to protest it, fought tooth and nail. I mean you wouldn't want to be on the wrong side of her in the first place. So why did she do that? Why would you fight so hard for it? And obviously, in the end, they didn't knock any of it down except the old garages and bin sheds. She won.'

She won, sure, except the old community halls were sold off to a private developer and the bike sheds are run by a company that leases you back your old space. But she won the garden. And it's impressive: rows and rows of raised beds, a small orchard, wild flowers and berry bushes in between. It looks beautiful. It looks like another place has broken out of the soil and torn a hole in the city.

'Like why else would she care so much about it? She's killed him and buried him under there. And the rest of the estate are too scared to go to the police.'

The waiter comes back to tidy up, and she wipes up the last of the oil and honey with the sourdough bread before she will let him take the plate. I want to order a bottle of red wine and drink too much of it.

'Okay, but do you eat the vegetables?'

'Yes, of course I eat them. Why not? It's all fertiliser. It's all organic, isn't it?'

I laugh because she wants me to, and because it's funny. It's silly. She wants to order the Chateaubriand. Of course she does. I go along with it like a wave is sweeping me away. I try to work out which card I can put my half on. She wants it bloody, even though the waiter says they serve it a particular way. It's undressed salad leaves all over again.

When the food comes I feel queasy looking at all the flesh. Thick slices of pink meat bending over one another in a blood-red puddle. I think about a guy I met on the tube. He went out of his way to sit next to me in an empty carriage, let his thigh press against mine and stared at the side of my face. I felt his eyes burning my cheek, and eventually I turned my head and took him in. He was maybe ten years older than me, and it wasn't that he looked bad, he didn't. He looked smart enough and normal enough. But his eyes looked like two giant pupils, like he was a dead body. And something about him set off this screaming instinct in my chest to get away. My whole body told me he was dangerous. He had brown hair in curtains and pale skin. He was dressed, I think, in an expensive suit. He smiled broadly and spoke to me in a way that I know should have been charming but for some reason none of that was working. I jumped out of my seat and practically ran to the other end of the carriage. My heart was in my mouth because it was empty and the next station felt like it would never arrive. I will never forget trying to slow my breath, trying to look straight ahead at the doors, all the while seeing him reflected in the glass. Him getting up, moving slowly, in no rush at all, to get me, deliberately taking each heavy step. His smile so fixed it looked like a grimace. Coming through the centre of the carriage, taking his time to get to me, stepping through until it was maybe three steps, two steps, a step left. And the train jerking to a stop at the station, and seeing people queueing by the door, and trying to prise the doors to open them faster as I jumped off, jerking my head back to look for him. And then I stood a few steps off the train on the platform, watching him as he leant his head out of the door, people pushing past him to get on and him not moving except to blow kisses at me. His eyes completely full of spite, his face without any warmth, blowing kisses.

In a city this big it makes sense that everything is happening somewhere. Anything you can think up is probably happening. Why wouldn't it be? Simply in terms of scale.

They find people who have been kidnapped and trafficked, don't they? You hear about normal families that are hell behind closed doors. I lived in a flat for years without realising the people in the basement were drug dealers. They were quiet and polite. Why wouldn't we be surrounded by killers? That's just the odd day in their lives; the rest of the time they need to catch the tube like everyone else. How close have I come to escaped war criminals or sex offenders?

By the time we are eating dessert, I have convinced myself that Sue is a murderer. I do these things because I am drunk and feeling reckless, but I let Tara think she's convinced me of them both. She wants a port and a coffee. I am imagining the bill leaping up in £20 increments. As she is sipping her port she finally focuses her big blue eyes on me and fluffs her hair behind her shoulders as she looks at me properly for the first time. It's time to steel myself for my turn to talk.

'So how are you? How are things with Steven? How's work?'

I am obsessed with a man at work who I desire so desperately that I cannot breathe properly around him. We meet up in the archive room in the basement of the school, underneath the office where I work, and I cannot believe that it is me doing this and that nobody has caught us. Every night I shower before Steven gets home and I told him I have joined a new gym. I feel alive and on fire and like I cannot trust anything I do. I have stopped ever feeling comfortable. I feel sick and exhausted and I don't dare do a pregnancy test. Last week I stole several hundred pounds' worth of identical cashmere jumpers from Marks & Spencer's. Two nights ago I walked silently to the kitchen and opened the drawer and picked up a sharp knife and held the blade in my hand, and if I was less of a pathetic suburbanite, I would have walked over to our bedroom and done what needs to be done, but instead I cut my palm and had to pretend at work I had broken a wine glass.

'Oh, you know me, not much to report. Same old, same old. We've booked to go to Latitude next year, so I'm looking forward to that.'

Tara rolls her eyes.

What You
Could Have Done

Turn the corner at the top of my road, start down towards the bus stop and there it is. *Even Superdads Aren't Invincible.* On the billboard, there he is.

It's not him, it's a model, but anyone who knows him would know it was him. I even texted him about it and we laughed about it. We both put 'haha' in the messages. And then I asked how he was and he stopped replying.

And every day at the top of the road as I start down to the bus stop, there he is. Even superdads aren't invincible. Him (not him) and his son (again, I know) on a sofa. The son dressed as the closest to Batman I guess you can have on an advert. And his face is kind of scrunched up and the child is clambering over him. Three or four, I would say. About the exact age. And they're both laughing. And behind them a window onto a garden. It's in a house, not a flat, even though he's only thirty-seven and how does anyone have that in London? No one who spends time with their children in the daytime has that.

And I swear I hadn't been thinking of him, hardly ever, and here I am going through the photos on my laptop after my boyfriend is in bed. Looking over my shoulder, not wanting to be caught out. Him and me. Trying to cry silently because the walls in this place are only there for decoration.

On the screen in front of me I am the most in love I have ever been. So bold and brazen and smug with it on a beach on the Île de Ré. The day after we both first said it. All of it documented, sun shining down. My head pressed against his chest in bliss. And understanding what bliss was, like two horses stood next to each other in a field.

We look young and we look bright and pure, saying: what we have is better than any of you have ever had and will ever have, light and free and younger and luckier than all of you, and we are having more and better sex than you've ever had. Sacred. Sickening and cute as fuck. And all the songs you love make better sense to us. For the first time and the best time.

I didn't realise that I still had that whole day memorised. I walk myself through it as slow as I can. The local bus over to the island. A coach with brown patterned seats. Carpet fabric scratching my bare legs. His hand stroking the back of my head. Driving by rich French people's summer houses, winding in and out of the sunlight. Putting on my sunglasses and posing. Walking to the harbour, the sun hitting the little white boats. Trying to find something to eat and not wanting to choose or go inside. Telling my friends the next week, 'We walked about, and we couldn't find anywhere! So in the end we just bought a couple of macarons, for our whole lunch!' as their eyes glazed over. The first young couple to go to France, the first young couple to fall in love, bringing back their Incredible Anecdotes.

And afterwards we got into the water on the stony beach and swam out to a little pontoon. Surrounded by old couples wading into the water in baggy old swimming costumes. Old French men looking like you'd hope. Smoking in the sea, looking like walruses. We raced each other, and the ladder had only one step up and he said to me, 'It's okay, baby, put both feet on, like when you're waterskiing.' And I laughed at him for being a posh boy, thrilled I had managed to make a posh boy fall for this shit.

I get into bed, and my boyfriend jumps out of his skin and cries out. 'It's just me, baby, it's just me, okay?' He's affronted. I try to hold him and he shakes me off.

So I lie still and I can't stop remembering now. That he noticed the awkward way I stand and said it was fifth position like a ballerina. That he said my neck was long and delicate. Me. This lumbering fucking beast over here. That I would call him when I was abroad for work and wake him up and his voice would be high and croaky, and without fail he would be so happy to hear me. That he actually liked how I was. And I would gaze at him. Just . . . gaze at him. As he closed his eyes and stretched his neck from side to side. As he cooked with the cricket on. As he did his receipts cross-legged on the floor. From our bed as he got dressed. As he slept.

It's too hot. I lie on the far edge of the bed, push the cover between me and my boyfriend and try to hold it in my arms.

The next day I'm late for the bus and I run down. Fuck off, mate, fuck you, why are you here? I say to him and his stupid fucking son as I pass the billboard. Fuck you, mate. The bus is packed and the condensation makes it feel like a greenhouse. I get a seat by apologising to someone sat in an aisle next to an empty window. I apologise again, and she stares me down. I get my phone out and I text him. I don't even think. My heart beats so fast, it's a thrill. I see him typing, and then it stops. I put my phone away because it frightens me.

I meet my friend Ellie for lunch by her office. I tell her I keep seeing one magpie everywhere I go. 'It's haunting me. It's killing me,' I say. She's impatient with me today. I tell her I'm serious and she tells me I need a hobby. Take up gardening, go back to the gym.

'Every time you see a magpie you think it means something?'

She's already laughing at me when I say yes.

'There are a lot of magpies about . . . so you see them about.'

She doesn't even look up from her plate, and I know I'm getting on her nerves. I texted Liam, I say. Why did you do that? she says. Because, I don't know, I say, giggling because I feel like I'm seven and I've been caught doing something naughty. She looks up and starts up with: 'I'm saying this because I care . . .'

In the afternoon he replies to me and it's like being hit in the chest. I sit with my phone on my knees, and he and I text back and forth, and I feel like I am somewhere completely different. I am not romanticising the past. I know I was unhappy. Sometimes. Look, I didn't know what unhappy meant then.

When I get home I am already stressed out by the time I open the front door. It's wedged again because it was raining this afternoon and the water has pooled underneath it onto the mat. There is a line of drowned ants up the hall. I hate the flat. I hated it when we walked round it and I hated it when I said let's go for it and I hate it more every single day. I lean against the wall and try to stop myself from crying. Why am I being so stupid? It's just that once I start thinking about it I can't get rid of how it feels. I miss my old place. I close my eyes and try to walk back through it. I want to walk back into one of the parties we threw and I want to live there.

My boyfriend is already home and in the kitchen. 'That you?' Obviously it's me. He wants to bicker about dinner. I go out to buy us a bottle of wine and I buy two. I try to get us both so drunk that I can't think about this, but I can't stop, even after he has called it a night.

I remember I have a file on my computer. I forgot I did this, but after I told Liam to leave I went round our flat, this new flat we both hated, that helped so well to break us up. And I took photos of his possessions, sat there in static like the *Mary Celeste*. Crime scene photos. His shoes all in a row. His watch by the side of the bed. His underwear. The little details of what he was just delighted me. A blue sweatshirt I was so attached to that I stopped it going to charity three times. The day I met him, he came to the chemist with me and we waited and got coffees. All documented. I cross-reference a photograph of him in front of the shop, a sign behind him, *2007 Is Here*, in a back-to-school display. 2007 is all still here. It won't let me go. A blue sweatshirt and him staring right down the lens, a little smile. A blue sweatshirt still on the floor, waiting to be washed like nothing had happened.

Before I go to bed I text him that I need to meet up with him. That I need to speak to him. I'm so drunk when I do it I don't even remember the next morning when I'm sitting on the bus to the tube, feeling wretched and trying not to be sick. I only notice because he has stopped texting me. I only notice because I'm desperate for him to text me.

He doesn't reply, over and over again, for hours and days on end. I snap myself out of it. Ellie says there's only so many times I can go away on my own and sit looking melancholy out of a train window before it starts reflecting badly on me. I try to live in the present. The present is a gift! It's a gift I lost the receipt for. I plant things in the front garden and I wait to feel better. Slugs eat them. I plant them in the kitchen, and then wait, and plant them out. Slugs eat them, but quicker.

It takes him a month to get back to me, and when he does it is so easy and so casual that no time has passed at all. He says it sounds like a great idea to meet up, that it's been a long enough time and that we should do it. The relief is like falling asleep.

He's already there, and the walk to the table to sit down is agony, I feel so self-conscious I am almost on tiptoes. I sit down, and there's such a friendly awkwardness between us before we really start speaking. We ask about each other's families and laugh in a knowing way at each other's answers. We order sparkling water because that's what we always did. He doesn't want to eat, which is fine, it's fine, it doesn't mean anything. It is lovely to be near him again. He is wearing the same fragrance he sprayed on a letter to me. I hope it is deliberate. Then there is a break where we have run out of recent things to say, and there's only what I have to say. Like walking up the steps to a high diving board, I'm still thinking I can't do it.

And once I start saying it all I can't stop crying. It just comes out so much that I am heaving trying to catch my breath. The waitress brings me a tissue and I joke that he has just dumped me. I joke that he is heartless not to be crying too, anything to try to stop myself making this stupid scene. I tell him, whispering, in between deep breaths, that I haven't stopped loving him.

I can't stop.

He doesn't say anything at all.

I stop myself crying. I try to make more jokes. 'We went to Japan for fuck's sake. That's like getting married for hipsters.' The joke just sits there.

Finally he starts talking to me again. 'Except it isn't getting married. I want you to know that after you left me it was like you had died. I didn't know how else to deal with it. It was the worst I have ever felt. And, yes, some part of me loves you, but . . . I don't want it to be dangerous to my life now. I've met someone and . . .'

'I live with my boyfriend,' I say. We are in the same boat, it's okay. We can end things and start again.

'. . . she's great. And I don't want to put that in danger.' He thinks I am here to have an affair.

I think I realise something right then. He thinks I am someone who has affairs. He thinks because of what I did that I didn't ever hold us sacred, that he didn't mean to me what he did, that I don't mean what I'm saying now.

'I know what I did was wrong, but I didn't even have it in me to talk properly then. Jesus, we didn't even row. That's not healthy. And I know what I did was wrong but I can't be punished for it forever.'

'You left me and you wouldn't speak to me.'

'I was so young and really stupid, and if I could do it now, I could do it so differently – I would do it so differently. I feel like I stopped being a good person back then. I don't want to move on: I want to fix it.'

I don't even know what happens after that. He starts talking about how our relationship taught him to communicate better, like our relationship was in the past. Like I'm just one of his exes. And then eventually we walk to the tube together, and it feels cordial, and like this was closure for a second, but it dissipates the second he goes. And then I am hyper-ventilating in a newly done-up toilet in King's Cross. It just cost me 30p to not be able to breathe. The automatic flush keeps automatically flushing behind me, and I'm gasping, and it hurts my chest. I say to myself: it was a mistake and it wasn't a mistake. It was a choice, it was a decision, I did something at least.

I thought that, if I left you, it would get better and easier. I left you, and it never got better or easier. When I decided, it's like I let sadness and trepidation in. I let doubt in and it crawled all over me. It finds me wherever I go.

Six months after I left, you emailed me. You said, 'Let's go for counselling. Time is running out for us to sort this out,' and I cried on the tube. And a woman held me as I got off, and said, 'I can stay with you if you need me to,' and I said that was very kind but I was okay. And I thought at my deepest level: 'How can I meet you when I've done all this? How can I look at you when I've been with someone else now?' And my pride hated how long you had taken. And I made myself think at a closer, louder level, 'I shouldn't go to counselling. I'm with someone else now. I look forwards and not back,' and I left it. But I was still so certain that I could get over anything, that I was invin-cible. I thought nothing could leave an impression on me that would last. I thought I could just keep running. But, honestly, in what universe am I a fast runner? In what universe am I a runner at all?

I am not drunk when I get off the bus and climb onto the little wooden balcony in front of the poster. I have never been much of a drinker anyway. I couldn't keep up with you. You were always out or away, and I hated the pub and pints and the football. I just wanted us to be on our own again, even though when it happened I didn't know what to say. It is really funny to me right now, standing on it and feeling how unsafe it is, that this poster has its own little balcony and I do not. I am right next to you again. Not you, I know. I start trying to hack at it, but it's got some coating on the print. It's fucking invincible! I get the Stanley knife out of my bag and try to cut myself a corner to pull off. There are a hundred posters underneath, a thick, hard wedge, and I can't get any purchase. I get the paint pot out of my bag, but it's a little tester one and it doesn't even cover your face. I was going to paint the outside wall like a rainbow and now I've painted half your face blue.

When I notice the police are there I am so terrified it's like I'm at school again. But they just ask me to get down and if I'm okay and is there somewhere they can take me? Is there someone they can call to collect me? I start feeling so angry I can't control myself. I am not a fucking charity case. I missed my chance. It is serious. Once I shout it at them, it's not serious: it's stupid, it's funny even. It's sad. It's pathetic. I'm lucky they don't think I'm a threat. I know I don't have anything to worry about. I'm sorry, I'm so sorry, I can't apologise enough. I am a bad person.

★   ★   ★

Days pass and weeks pass, and they finally take that haunted fucking picture down. They replace it with an advert for a fertility clinic, and I have to admire the joke.

I am coming home from work with two bottles of wine. A couple is sat opposite me on the tube, with a brochure from the same place. 'It's out of our control, isn't it?' he tells her. 'There's no use worrying, that'll just make it worse,' he tells her.

I close my eyes and I say a prayer. Oh God, if I am ever lucky enough to love and be loved again, I won't fuck it up, I swear I won't fuck it up. Please.

In the night I wake up and I shout out in the dream I was having.

My boyfriend says, 'Don't worry. You're safe now, you're with me now.'

Poets Rise Again

'I would give anything, anything, if I could have grown up with a father who loved me and a mother who wanted me around. It's like people look at me and all they can see is this idea of me, that I have this charmed life, but it's not fair, it's not fair.' She starts crying again, and Naomi squeezes her arm and passes her a little pack of tissues. It takes a long time to open them. We both sit, watching her try to get the little plastic flap up and pull a tissue out, and then loudly blow her nose onto it and put it on the desk so, so close to my goddamned arm.

'I'm sorry. I know to you it's just poor little rich girl . . .
I know, I'm sorry . . . I have felt guilty my whole life. I
just can't cope.'

Naomi looks at me, but I swear to God I am going to
start laughing just out of nerves and I shake my head, so she
starts up. 'We know. It's so hard to' – she pauses and flashes
me a look, like help me out here, and I flash back, like
babe I'm out of my depth also – 'change your circumstances
in life . . .' Naomi swallows back something like disgust.
'. . . For everyone. That's what people don't appreciate.'

'Thank you. I can't help that I've been fortunate. I'm a
good person.'

That tissue is nearly touching the hairs on my arm, I swear.

'I'm not a bad person.'

Okay, time for me to speak for the first time. 'We know.
We don't think that.'

'At all,' Naomi chimes in – thank you – in sync.

After two hours we both hug her and she leaves. We
wave to her, not smiling, not anything, just calm as the
school nurse giving you an injection, as she passes by outside
the office. Our first customer. Three. Thousand. Fucking.
Pounds. I can't stop laughing. We're jumping up and down.
She's just the first of ten bookings this week.

I go home, get changed, kiss my mummy on the forehead
and go straight back out to meet Nems. We are going for
dinner and we are not going to think about the money. I
order us cocktails and a bottle of wine. I don't want there
to be any time in the meal where we have less than two
drinks each. Yes, we are paying the supplement for cheese

or steak or lobster or whatever fancy shit costs the supplement, thank you. We are going to get dessert wine, fuck it.

'Naomi, this is the beginning,' I say for a toast. 'When you started this scheme, I will admit I had my doubts. I had my doubts . . .' I'm trying to make this something we can remember, I want it to be official. 'But look at this, look at us. We are fully fledged, we have taken our maiden voyage and the world is ours!' We are so loud that people are staring at us, but I think they'd be staring at us anyway. Unfortunately my new money is as good as yours, mate. And we look fucking beautiful. Two bright birds of paradise.

We are eating little butterscotch puddings and drinking hot liqueur coffee cocktails, when Nems looks so serious and leans in. 'This isn't even it, you know? This is just the first floor, the entry level. Yes, we can get this money absorbing all their feelings and, yes, we can build up our client base and, yes, we can run retreats and workshops, and you can bet, yes, I am going to be adding two zeros onto everything we do when we go to Kensington and Chelsea and Richmond, trust me. But this isn't even it. I'm talking about getting these people to give it up. Properly give it all up. And thank us for it.' She downs the last bit of drink and winks at me, and we both crease up. Got to be dramatic when you do these things, otherwise what life are you living?

And that is how the plan was made. In between dessert and the hot mint tea where I spent most of the time looking into the water to see if there were bugs in it so we could get it for free. She says we don't need to do that, do we? But I will always love a bargain. I gave a card to a sour-faced old couple as we left. She did a double take like she was trying to suppress real terror as I came over. Then she did some kind of facial dance as she read it. I watched her all the while, so I could give her the warmest smile I could, and then I walked out like I was prime minister. Like I was a cruise ship. Stately as a galleon, I thought to myself.

Confidence is something you can practise. You can practise at home, in the mirror. You can practise to yourself as you go to bed at night. You can develop your persona for public speaking and you can use it whenever you need to. That's what was drummed into us. When we were in sixth form, Nems and I were in the debate team. The legendary year where our school, our shitty school, Our Lady of Perpetual Help, cleaned the fuck UP. Without over-bragging, with perhaps just a lovely bit of bragging, me and Nems *were* the debate team. It was our pair that won the three competitions. The B-team, Elaine Nicholson and Clara Stevens (I will never forget their full names and I will only ever call them their full names), were dead wood. We carried those timid little mice as they stumbled their way alongside us.

Our sixth form was the only time where Our Lady even had a debate team. It coincided with the reign of Mr Hunter in the History Department. He was involved, I now think, in one of those teach-first-fuck-off-later schemes. He wore a cravat and a hat to school. He was probably twenty-five but that was just 'old' back then. He had permanent red cheeks, although was otherwise very pale, and looked like a porcelain doll, but one with a trimmed beard and styled moustache. He was short, five foot five maybe, but he had presence. And he loved to speak. And he loved the idea of getting us to fuck over the private schools. And we loved that too. It was an instant bond. He would sit with us in the library with the *Economist* and the *Guardian* and the *Telegraph*, telling us what it all signified. Cramming. Giving us practice topics and cue cards. He wanted us to win so much that once he screamed at little mouse Elaine after she couldn't remember her points and nearly lost us our place in the rotary final. Which, of course, me and Nems then smashed. It was a joke with us that the school had to build a trophy cabinet for our trophies. Each time we won he'd say, 'They'll have to put a new shelf up now, girls.'

Extracurricular is what got me into Cambridge, I have no doubt. It got Nems into Durham, and it got Mr Hunter into whatever graduate scheme he disappeared into. And I tried debating once I got there, but it wasn't the same without her. Or him. I didn't want to do it on my own. I couldn't win.

It got us in, but after that it just left us there. And when I arrived there I needed a break. It had taken all my strength to be the prize pony, and still look after Mum at home, and earn, and hide it all. And that's the opposite of what the rest of them were doing. I know I should have got there and kept swimming, but I was exhausted. They hit the ground running, and I hit the wall, and that was that. Nems did better, because she always does. Some people have magic to them. It's like they breeze through life and it works for them. It's like they are playing a better version of this game. I am not one of those people. And sometimes the allure of it makes me want to be with her, hang on to the coattails, and sometimes it makes me want to punch her.

But all of this, it makes me treasure her. I would follow her to the ends of the earth for making this work. She sorted the office, rent-free, for a year. All we had to do was give a presentation to the board of the charity that runs this place. Put up a new shelf, girls. And it's not even her main hustle. She did this for us. For me.

It's not even much, but I have really made it work for us. The room is dim, so we made it cosy. We put up pictures of people who they would find inspiring but not threatening. Malala, Martin Luther King, Buddha, Stacey Solomon. Our desks are to one side – totally artificial, we don't do admin here, really, but we want to give the impression of busy, smart people taking time out to help. It's like a therapist's room, but with softer furnishings. 'It has to feel as safe as the womb,' Naomi declared when we were working out the decor. We aren't doing the Good Lord's work here. We are taking their money. Make no bones about it. We don't have the time in our lives to make them understand, and even if we did, it wouldn't pay enough to compensate us.

First time we tried to flex into the new idea we lost a client over it. It's not an easy shift, and we tried it too fast. A fifty-year-old, twice-divorced dad. He looked so good for it though. He looked styled every time he came in. In good shape. Everything about him screamed money, and he thought it did the opposite. Scruffy hair, in excellent condition. Beat-up backpack that I googled and cost four hundred pounds. I counted thousands of pounds that made him look so understated. He skateboarded in the first time he came, and that alone made me want to try it out on him. It was his first time seeking any sort of help, and he had been coming for a month. He had come on to each of us separately, so I think he had his own goals too.

He was talking, at length, about how angry he was that his first ex-wife wanted to use their house in France all summer. He didn't even want to keep the place on. It was a burden. The magic word!

'Okay,' I said, 'just as a thought experiment' – thought experiments are, after all, the heart of a debate – 'playing devil's advocate here: what if you just gave it to her?' I'm hoping I know what's going to come next, and it does.

'Give it to her? I'd sooner cut my balls off and post them to her. No, she's the last person on earth I would give it to.'

'Then give it to us,' Naomi said.

It hung there for a second, and I looked at Naomi. We were way out on a limb, but you never know.

He laughed. He sat up on the couch. He looked at us like he was trying to figure us out, and then something clicked and he regained his composure. My blood ran cold. He started speaking to us in the false, jovial way he did that first time he met us, that we had gently worked at getting him to shed. That way he used to assure us that he is absolutely the same as us and that he is not racist or sexist or classist, that he is exactly on a level with everyone. The way my posh boyfriend at uni would talk to cab drivers, the only time in his life he said 'mate' and talked about football. He left the session early, and when I sent him his next appointment reminder he politely cancelled. A week later Naomi sent me a link to a song he'd put up on his godawful SoundCloud about trust. The thrill, the fear, the abject terror of being rumbled. But thank God someone like him would never want to make that humiliation public. It was a warning shot to do things with a much lighter touch.

The next time, we pitched it as a kind of CBT-style thing, to try, just to try, just to see if it helped things feel easier. We asked Olivia, who had spent every session saying she wanted to branch out on her own, just to try diverting the support her father gave her each month, just for a couple of months, so she didn't have to feel beholden to him. We arranged for her to stay in Naomi's sister's spare room. She managed two weeks before we got a phone call, direct from the man himself.

We tried and tried, and I was starting to feel like it would never happen. 'They don't actually want to lose out. They just want it hidden, not taken. They want the stuff, not the guilt. We know this.'

Naomi's eyes lit up. 'So we have to better link the guilt to the stuff!' I could see her again at school, first hand up every single time. Prefect, head girl, every possible little badge. Every single pat on the head she could get, then taking the piss out of it all with me on the bus home. She looked at me like 'We know this. This is a game to work out how to win.'

We spent a week drawing up the rules. We had to make it very clear that we were to tell them that we were just administrating the takeover of assets. Not because we wanted the money. If we want the money, then they think we are envious, and they all hate that. If we want the money, then they want the money too. Or at least they want the money to make sure nobody else gets it.

The first try, we get a Range Rover. I am not even joking.

We get a car, and its previous owner is fucking elated to be getting the bus. He keeps calling us, saying he's never felt so normal. He emails us an anecdote about the conversation he had with the lady sat next to him. I think it had been years since he'd spoken to a stranger who wasn't a waiter. I don't even dare look up how much it is worth. He fucking signs it over to us, and he laughs as he does it. He signs it over to Nems because I can't drive, but that is a moot point, and as I point out to her, it makes her my de facto chauffeur.

A week later we drive it to Imogen's holiday home in Cornwall, as she is no longer going to be using it this summer. She is going to a caravan park, and she's so excited she's started an Instagram about it: @myrealsummerfamily.

Six hours driving, with me and Nems in the front laughing and bopping away and Mummy in the back asking questions. Mum is tense in ten different ways. The last time we went away somewhere, I was tiny. I don't even know when she last left London that wasn't just a day to visit some old family up north somewhere.

'Which friend from university, Naomi? Which friend is this? Have I met them? And they're not needing it? They really don't need it? And you are sure about this? And this car – oh, you've done so well for yourself.' Mum falls asleep, smiling and contented. She's pleased with me by extension.

It goes without saying that this is the biggest house I can remember setting foot in. Imogen has organised for the chef to come. When she mentioned it I flashed a look at Nems and she smiled to confirm that, yes, neither of us had a clue that these places came with staff, and that, yes, we had narrowly avoided the fuck-up of Imogen knowing that too. If we don't understand how things are done, we can't be a safe pair of hands.

We stay for three weeks. I want to get used to it. Every morning the chef, Maureen, puts on coffees and we sweep downstairs and drink them looking out at the bay. Nems wears sunglasses in the house and calls me dahling. Mum can't get into it, and evenings she's in the kitchen trying to help out, determined that she won't have anything done for her. Maureen is about her age, and by the last week she's just given up. Mum cooks with her, then they sit up chatting together.

The little cove that belongs to the house is pretty, but you have to climb down to it, so Mum mostly sits out by the pool and waves at us. I don't know if I've ever seen Nems in water, but one night after dinner we get over-excited and jump into the sea, screaming and yelping at the cold and how it takes your breath away. And I can't stop saying, 'But it was so hot today!' like I will not believe how the night works, and Nems is just flat-out laughing at me and trying to float, so she can look up at the stars. So many stars – it's like there's a VIP room for stars I didn't know about – and fresh air and water. I have to check myself because I'm in it, and I'm staying in it.

After we get home it is like we have brought something back with us. We buy so many new clothes, and our focus is on the quality of the fabrics and what to wear alongside each other. We update the website. We spend a week looking for venues to host our retreats, and every single one we show up at treats us like the real deal. They look us up and down and nod their heads and take us on tours like we should be going on tours.

I come up with the best idea during a session with Amelia, mid-divorce from a Tory MP. The more she says his name, the more I remember the sex scandal, but I try not to let it register on my face. We aren't doing well with her, and out of nowhere I say, 'I know what it's like to be where you are, because, believe it or not, I was in your position once.'

Naomi raises her eyebrows like, okay, girl, you enjoy yourself, let's see where this goes. She's used to me impro-vising, and I think she likes the challenge. We are getting good at this, so let's see how much fun we can have, she's thinking.

'Before I met Naomi at Cambridge . . .' I can't resist getting in anti-Durham jabs when she can't fight back.

'Okay,' Naomi says, licking a smile off her lips.

'. . . before I met Naomi, there wasn't a single part of my life that felt real or authentic to me. I never fitted in at school, and when I was home for the holidays, I don't have to tell you how lonely that can be. It doesn't matter how beautiful the place in Capri is, does it?'

Nems has moved to looking concerned, holding her pencil, and I know she is loving this.

'I didn't know what a normal life was. I just knew that I wanted it, that I wanted to . . . step away from the loneliness and the frigidity and the dysfunction of the world around me. I didn't want to feel guilty anymore and I wanted to build my own life, for myself.'

Amelia is staring at me with a kind of devotion, like I've converted her.

'Are you a Buddhist, Amelia?'

We talk a bit about how the world you can see is the world you create, but how she could create an entirely different one. We talk so gently, on tiptoes, about how having less is having more. About how giving is receiving.

The next week Amelia is on one. She emails me every day, just me, which Nems cannot get over. She wants to make a plan. She wants to try and convert some friends too. She wants to come on the retreats and she thinks I should write a book. I strategise with Nems about how to handle this flood of engagement. I think she wants a project; Nems thinks she just wants a friend. Either way, we want to encourage her and lead her to her own ideas – her own ideas being the ones we need to give her.

She has been paying us a retainer for four months when one day she tells me that she needs to get rid of everything. I lean back at my desk and press both of my palms against my face. I didn't think we would get here for years, and I always thought it would be an older guy out to get revenge on his children or something. I didn't think it would be her.

We arrange an emergency session with her, just to test the waters. We both wear linen dresses because I want her to think of it like a religious experience. When she arrives in reception I hug her and act like I'm trying not to cry. In reality I'm barely keeping a lid on all of this. We are so close to stepping up and we know it.

In the dim light we talk to her about unburdening herself and what that would mean. About how whatever we would administrate would then become a part of our organisation, which, as she knows, is set up on Buddhist principles to help as many people as possible. We talk about how she could potentially (keep it far off and uncertain, please) run retreats for us. I talk about her spirit. She goes through her various sources of income. Her assets. She is sure she can't remember them all, and she is sure that her soon-to-be ex wants to get his hands on whatever he can. She spits his name.

'Your spirit is so bright,' I say, stroking her hand.

The thing that strikes me is how hard it is. We have to split into two teams for her. Nems is on the new life and I'm on the old. Every time Naomi organises her a holiday or tries to talk to her about a regular job, I swear to God this woman bounces onto her feet like a cat. Everyone wants her on a board of something, everyone wants her at their summer house. We are only trying to get her just to normal – it's not even like we are trying to make things hard – but the money saves her every time. She can't fail downwards. I feel like if she went to prison it would have a tennis club.

I make a little more progress, but it's slow and it does my head in. There is another reason I didn't finish my law degree, and it's because it's dry as the Sahara desert. It feels physically like my will to live is being scraped out, even when I know the prize is winning the lottery. The ex-husband's maintenance can be diverted to our organisation. We can work on getting the house signed over to us. Same with some of her passive income. We can meet up and talk about her savings too.

At the next session she says she admires nurses, so we set a nurse's income as her ideal budget to live on. We can administer it from her maintenance and help her learn to live on it. Only after she leaves do I see that Nems is almost shaking with anger. She's never usually the one to get annoyed, so it almost frightens me to see her like it. I hadn't been thinking; her mum is a nurse.

'She wants to play dressing-up? Fuck her. Fuck her.'

But then we start to laugh because what the fuck have we created? We are paying her not to be a nurse.

'When is she going to catch a fucking clue though?' she says after a minute.

The two or three or, honestly, God knows weeks pass by where I'm losing the plot because all I can do is sit with Mum and try to make her comfortable while we wait all day, every day, for a cancellation at the free clinic. The whole time I'm stroking her hair and trying to make her more comfortable on the plastic leather chairs that make you sweat and slide slowly off. I can barely sit still. I just keep thinking there's something I can do. I keep going back to reception, like a fly diving against a window.

I keep thinking about the shock after I tried to take her to a private clinic. Walking in like 'this is it, we VIPs now' and sitting in the reception and being brought a coffee and a water each. The place done up somewhere between a hotel and a spa and quiet and empty. And then the doctor so attentively telling us everything we already know. And then showing us the treatment options where the scale of the money felt like they were adding zeros for fun. And trying to work out how I can tell Nems that we've got to speed shit up, and knowing she wouldn't risk it, and knowing she's right that it wouldn't work, but this desperate feeling like I'm in a horror film trying every key in the door and it won't open.

All this money coming in, and I can't even speed up her getting an ID. I tried to get myself on health insurance, but even with that they won't touch me because of her status, and because I can't prove this income is forever. I'm dropping the keys on the floor and the murderer is coming up behind me.

And all the while I'm having to text my fucking 'friend' Amelia, who is upset she's having to budget to buy food and upset that she's realised Waitrose is expensive and upset that buying a coffee eats into your money, and I want to call her and shout at her. I try to find it funny, but it's one too many things for me to process. I am just about keeping my head above water – there can't be another thing.

And of course the other thing decides it's the perfect time to ring the doorbell, doesn't it! Naomi calls me in to the office and I have to go. We sit next to each other with Amelia's sister on speakerphone. How am I this stunned she found us? We're not hiding; that's the point. At first, Cordelia just asks us about the retreats and if we offer counselling. I look at Nems, and I can feel us building up to ace this. She smiles at me like we have nothing to fear here. She is appropriate and charming, and talks about our duty of care, the importance of confidentiality.

I can almost hear Cordelia eating it up, until she speaks again. 'I need to check that she's been honest with you . . .' she says, in a way that I can't divine. That's the hard part: it's like we are learning a different emotional language. The reservedness, the curtness, the friendliness even – the rules are all different. They sound like politicians. They are the politicians, I guess.

'My sister struggles with her mental health. She's bipolar, yeah? She's had several psychotic breaks, yeah? She's struggled with addiction . . . with you bloody name it, yeah?' She sounds angry, but not with us, and I think about Amelia, who has only ever really been sweet and earnest and alone.

'The whole family has struggled. My father can't cope with it anymore. Anyway. It looks like she's on another bender, and I need to know what your organisation is doing to help her.'

I take a breath and I dive in, aware of how I am pronouncing every word: 'At our organisation, our sole focus is on making our clients feel happier and more able to live a life that is authentic to them and their needs. It's a therapeutic organisation, but we are here to provide coaching on a more practical level too.'

'And are you aware of her medical history?'

Naomi jumps in: 'No, that's not something she's chosen to disclose to us.'

'Right, but you're counselling her – don't you have a right to her medical history?'

I hear Nems swallow. 'That's not how we operate.'

I hear a click on the line and I brace myself for something.

'What are your credentials, actually? Where did you qualify?'

I look at Nems, and she looks at me like, how do we play this? And I don't know. I don't know. It's like everything has slowed right down and I remember at uni when they asked me 'Where did you go to school?' and I didn't even realise I wasn't answering their actual question until it was too late.

'We understand that you're concerned about your sister, but we are here to work with her, and part of that contract is that we maintain her confidence – that we take her side in things.'

Did I say that or did Naomi? Where did it even come from?

I do not have the space in my mind to worry the way Nems is. It just seems clear to me now. We have to make sure the family don't get in our way, so we get her to cut them out. And I am genuinely sure that's best for her too. When Amelia shows up looking fucked and wired and saying she can't pay for counselling anymore it doesn't stress me. I tell her there is always money. There has to be.

I just want to be with my mum. None of this feels real or important anymore; it's just something we have to finish so that I can pay to get her treated. When Amelia calls and says she can't cope and she's crying and ranting down the phone it sounds like I'm listening to a car radio that isn't tuned in.

I hadn't really noticed the change in Naomi until she starts at me, immediately one morning, like she's attacking me while I've barely made my coffee. I am still putting the pod into the new machine, still choosing my creamer sachet – it feels uncivilised to have her come at me like this.

'Don't you feel any sympathy for them?'

I don't know what to say. I don't feel anything.

'She's going to lose their home!' Naomi keeps going, she sounds so desperate.

'Yes.' That's all I can say.

We both sit there, staring each other down. Heavy nose-breathing. Nothing.

Shrug.

'She's got kids!'

'Yes,' I say, shaking my head. *Yes. So.*

'They've had to leave their school.'

'Plenty of people we know had to move school when their parents got evicted. That's what being normal is. How else will she ever know?'

'Oh, come on. It's not because of her though, is it?'

'It is . . . It isn't . . . Look, honestly? I don't know. It sort of is. It's true enough. My mum is fucking dying. She is dying. And, fuck, she slept on the sofa of that flat for ten fucking years so I could have a room and what have I done to show for it? What happens if we don't do this?'

Now Naomi is silent. She's annoyed, and she keeps shaking her head, trying to form the right thing to say and then stopping.

'Nems, we won't ever fucking catch up with them. Life is too fucking short to play a game that's not fair. It's rigged from the start. We couldn't educate ourselves out of it and we can't do it just taking little bites.'

'Stop giving me a little speech. It wasn't supposed to be this . . . or . . . maybe I didn't think it through, okay? I just thought about us pulling it off. But this woman is sick. She's really not in her right mind and her kids are going to get hurt. It's too . . . I don't want to be a bad person. I need to be able to look myself in the mirror here.'

Ah, fuck you, I think. Fuck your jammy little life. Fuck you, at Christmas, with your nice parents. I am trying not to cry, and it's making my throat and my neck ache and ache and ache. If I try hard enough, I can push it all back down and I can feel calm and numb.

'She is dying. We are all disposable and nobody gives a shit.' Am I giving a speech? I don't know.

'I know you are struggling right now,' she starts, like a politician.

'You don't have a fucking clue.' My voice is shaking now.

'Don't start this with me. I know you've always thought I have it easier. Just because my parents have that little crumb more. It's a little fucking crumb. And you've forgotten what it was like for me at Durham? The amount of times I called you crying? You really don't know what it's like for me, even now? I didn't have the luxury of dropping out, and I don't have the luxury of getting a criminal record. It's my family that gets blacklisted, gets deported, not yours . . . I mean . . . I'm sorry about your mum too. But there's still lots of options we can find for her together. It's not the end – we don't have to give up.'

I don't know how long passes and I don't reply.

'But we don't need to go this far is all I'm saying.' She knows I'm not going to change my mind. 'I want to step back. Let's just go back to what it was. You said it yourself: all they want is to pretend, they only want to be tourists, and they don't really want to lose anything.' She takes a breath and stands herself up straighter. 'So let them pay us, pay us well, to give them a guided tour, but why does it have to go this far? We could actually do some good. We're making good money.'

'Good money isn't enough to do fuck all.'

She knows I'm not going to change my mind, and I have not seen her this distressed, maybe ever. She packs up her laptop, takes a few personal things off her desk and walks out. She won't even look at me, and I'm glad because I don't want to look at her. Pathetic little mouse.

I remember at school, right in the middle of our GCSEs, a girl, Michaela Bailey, stole a bottle of brandy from her dad and brought it in. After an exam the three of us sat and drank it in the wasteland behind the school. We were rolling drunk. Screaming-laughing-vomiting-rolling drunk. And then somehow we were back in school, in the head-master's office. In that way when you're drunk and you suddenly arrive in a new scene, lurching in. And I turn my head to see Naomi is sober and her uniform is smart and she is wriggling out of it. Brushing the dirt off her shoulders and readjusting her posture and walking out of the office, and I am too paralytic to do anything but watch her go. She doesn't look back, and the door shuts behind her.

It turns out that Nems should have warned me in her little speech that our legal standing wasn't as safe as we had thought. I shouldn't have dropped out of my law degree, it turns out. And of course I didn't take into account what money can always do, because it is starting to be very clear that I won't ever know that.

Amelia's brother-in-law works for *The Times*, I do know that. And that he must have made it his pet project to look into us. I used to hate that she thought I was her friend, but it hurts just as if she was when I find out that Amelia chose her sister over me.

I didn't take into account what someone who has always wanted a cause will do once they get one. How Amelia contacted every single one of our clients. How Amelia contacted her old friends to write about it. How Amelia convinced her ex-husband to speak in fucking Parliament about it, talking about dishonesty like butter wouldn't melt. Amelia making it into an online campaign. Amelia on *This Morning* making Holly Willoughby cry. She really worked hard to fight injustice when she was personally affected, credit where it's due.

And then it's just something hitting me every day. Nothing is a surprise, but every blow lands. The charity kicks us out of the office. Naomi will not speak to me. The arrest. The newspapers. The legal fees that eat up every penny of money I have ever made.

Mum dying.

Losing the flat. Losing my waitress job.

The trial.

On the steps of the court, I see Nems with her family all around her, and she won't even look at me. I walk in on my own, trying to go over what I want to say, prepping my points. I think of the day we won the national schools final. This House Believes We Are All Middle Class Now. Won by Our Lady of Perpetual Unfairness. Can you imagine? This house believes in absolutely nothing at all. This house believes nothing means anything anymore.

Between

It was my second pregnancy, and I was at the stage where I had started hallucinating. Everything felt a little too lucid. I was at the point where it's a gruelling, moaning effort to turn over at night. Sleeping only lightly and my mind not calming down. Up several times to pee, full of resentment as I hobbled round the bed and to the bathroom. Without any effort, the floor tiles became whole animated scenes acting themselves out in front of me, shifting and rippling like I was tripping. I didn't need to try. When I looked at a towel, a little face would stare back at me from its fibres.

I would close my eyes and shake my head, only to see it again, even more defiant when I opened them.

Have you ever had it where you think there's a fly on the ceiling and it's moving ever so slowly, but when you get up there to check, it's just a dot or a hole or a smudge, not alive, not at all? I would prop myself up on my back and just stare, gormless and bug-eyed at the ceiling above me. On the left-hand side I could see someone small in the cornicing, a little man trying to climb a rope to safety. Some nights he was higher up, other nights he wasn't there at all. On the right-hand side was something more frightening. Some nights there was a little girl drinking a bottle of Coke through a straw. I could see she was in a field, and that she was leaning backwards. Some nights it wasn't a bottle of Coke; it was that she was playing a clarinet or something like that. Some nights she was a praying mantis. But she was never totally still. Some nights it felt like I could see the wind on the cornfield behind her. Other ones I could feel it was stifling and hot.

I got so frightened of the dark. I had long since kicked Luke out into Katie's room on account of his snoring, even just his breathing disturbing and overheating me, and I didn't want to tell him how terrified I now was. The bed was so big. I stared into the shadows at the corners of the room and could not convince myself that there was nothing there. Or more that I couldn't convince myself, be one hundred per cent sure, that something wouldn't come. I felt so keenly vulnerable, that if I let myself sleep, anything could get me and the baby. You can't tell me for certain that I am safe, just like you can't tell me for certain there won't ever be a ghost or a demon or something. My heart could just stop and I'd never wake up. The sun has come up every day until now, but that isn't proof for tomorrow.

The days were a write-off. I would drift out of conversations and not notice I was kind of nowhere. I felt bovine. Sat on the sofa letting Katie stand right next to the TV to watch twenty episodes of her shows instead of two. Zoning out while she tried to tell me important things she had half learned and half made up. Only coming to when she started asking me, 'Did you know that, Mummy, okay?' I sat in that fog every day for weeks, and only felt alert once the rest of the house was asleep.

It feels like it was a long time, months and months, but that can't be true. My shuffling body felt slower than normal. Always too hot, always out of breath just going up the stairs. And then I got some kind of fever. Kids are little incubators for bugs and nursery makes you sitting ducks. They come out of it fine. You are floored. And I was half floored already. It lingered and took hold in me until I couldn't even leave the bed. And the bed was growing. It was twice the size it used to be, shoved up against the wall under the eaves, so that getting off was like climbing out of a rowing boat. It wasn't even worth trying half the time.

Luke was very good, bringing me meals and lemon and honey with no decent medicine in it, after I was scared off Lemsip by the internet. Katie would be ushered in like a little Victorian after supper. She started to look scared of me. She tried to clamber on top of me, elbowing me in the bump and then darting away when I howled in pain. She would be clinging on to her daddy as the howl turned into hacking and coughing my lungs up. He would awkwardly usher her out, trying to reassure me. Then I would be alone, on edge, checking the baby was okay, prodding them, bothering them, changing angle so I could put my bump onto my arm and make them move some more.

Sitting in bed, looking up at that woman reclining in a porch swing, the heat stifling the cornfield behind her, I realised that I hadn't left the house in ten days. Suddenly I was desperate for air. Slowly, I managed the climb out of bed and padded over to the window. It had been a week since I'd lifted the blind, and when I did the streetlights felt as bright as the sun. The air felt as fresh as if it had been raining. It felt wonderful. I just stood watching the street below. It was late, but we live in the city, and the city is always alive. Two teenagers playing basketball in the park, the clang of the ball hitting the tall metal fences, a man waiting for his dog to catch him up as it sniffed the base of every tree on the pavement, a cloud moving across the moon. I started crying because, I don't know why, but it started to feel really good, like a balm.

It was when I stepped away from the window and rolled down the blind that I started to hear a new noise. At first I thought it was just ringing in my ears. I've had that on and off for decades and I'm used to it, but after a while I couldn't deny that it was coming from outside me. I decided to go to the bathroom to pee; I was up already, I might as well. As I opened the door the sound was so loud it was like a fire rushing into the room. It wasn't quite buzzing, or humming, or static; it was all of them at once and something else altogether. It was so intense that I felt the blood pumping in my temples. How were Luke and Katie not woken up by it too?

Walking across the hallway scared me even more than usual. Usually, I imagine a hand suddenly on my shoulder or a figure behind me. I can imagine anything, and then I need to bat it away with a wave of my phone torch just to be certain that I am safe. This time I practically run into the bathroom and slam on the light as I bolt the door behind me. But the noise is worse in there. Sat on the toilet, I notice it is coming from the boiler cupboard opposite me. I can see the bright light seeping through the door frame.

I don't feel frightened anymore. It feels familiar to me, and I can't work out why. Have you ever had it where you have déjà vu that is so fleeting and so subtle that it feels like a memory of a dream? Or a memory of something you invented within the story of a dream? I try to work out why it's familiar and if it's real, but it's gone before I start, like it's fallen through my fingers. When I walk over to it I feel stronger with every single step.

The handle is burning hot in my hand.

Little timid knocks behind the bathroom door. Little timid knocks that are persistent. Then Luke's voice, a stage whisper: 'Are you alright? Did it wake you up too?'

Am I awake?

Suddenly, I am opening the bathroom door instead.

'Did it wake you?'

'The . . . noise?'

'Yeah, on the street? I think some kids were having a screaming match, but they didn't need to send five police cars, eh?' He sounds like he is underwater. 'I'm amazed Katie's still down. How are you feeling? Are you getting any rest? Are you feeling any better?'

He helps me back to bed. Above me the little man is gone. Has he climbed away? The woman is reclining, but her face is on fire. I fall asleep on my back and wake up a minute later, terrified that I have hurt the baby.

The next night I make sure I am not disturbed. I don't wait for it to call me. I go straight there. My hand on the door handle, my breath deep and assured. Like doing yoga in a sauna. Deep breaths that burn my nostrils. I hear the static whisper to me like it's calling a cat.

When I open the door I can see Katie being born. The absolute beautiful relief after it was done. I can see her open her eyes and look at me as they hand her to me. She is as small as a mouse, but she is five years old already and talking to me as I hold her. She is telling me about the mummy she had before she was born. Am I drugged? I had so much gas and air. I am fifty years old, I am sixty years old, I can see Luke telling me it will all be okay when I am talking with the doctor. I am sitting at primary school picking a scab on my arm, thinking: this moment is significant, I will remember this moment for a long time. The rows of book boxes in front of me, the little plastic bucket chairs. I am gasping for air, lying on my back screaming to wake up.

I am awake, it is the afternoon, and I am eating soup with parsnips in it. I am holding Katie as I read to her, I am feeling for the baby, holding my breath until she prods me away. Where am I?

I haven't checked the time, but when I enter the bathroom the moon is screaming in through the skylight and I see where she is on her journey across the sky. When I was trying to conceive for the second time I prayed to a fertility goddess because there was nothing else I could do. I found her name in a book but no other details about her. Onuava. Onuava, protect my baby, Onuava, I beseech thee. I repeated these words in my mind over and over. I called her up, hoping that, long forgotten, she wouldn't be busy. That she could travel up from the ground to our street, to our block of flats, built over thousands of years of forgotten magic. I made an image of her to pray to. A woman in the woods with long white hair. I tried to imagine her face, but it was blank.

Now I can see her looking down at me from the skylight, her clawed hands clinging on to the window frame. She is not calm. She is fierce and cruel, her eyes are bloodshot and she's salivating. She is reaching for my stomach. I sprint to the door and I open it.

I step inside and I am on a precipice. I am watching the sun rise from space. A thin little line of every single colour in the distance. A spark igniting in the vastness of the dark. It is as silent as the grave. I don't think I am even breathing.

Something small punches me in the back. It punches me again. Little timid knocks that are persistent.

And the door opens behind me, and Luke is there, panicked, Katie behind him rubbing her eyes. Are you okay? You're bleeding. I put my hand between my legs. He calls the ambulance.

It is a bright and beautiful afternoon, and I am sitting up in the hospital bed holding little Rosie. This morning they removed the catheter and the cannula and all their various wires and drips. Luke pours me a glass of water from the jug and smiles at me. He gets up to leave the room. It is just me and her, and I drink her in. I am awake. I am fine. I hear him joking with the midwife about finding me in the airing cupboard. This small man who has only lived in this one place, who has no idea.

A Photo Taken
at a Small-Town Museum

As we drove up it started to snow. I've never seen snow approaching in advance before, like a curtain. It was an accident, but the beat of the music on the stereo sped up. It was like we were watching a TV turn on. Old-fashioned static. And all the while we were curving round on the mountain road. I didn't drive then, so I didn't realise how frightening it was for you. You would never have let me know. You just stayed cool and quiet, and I stared at the snow curving inwards to hit us, waiting for the wiper to clear it.

When we got to the viewpoint we could not see a thing. You walked a couple of feet away from me and off the face of the earth. The next thing, you stepped out of nowhere and you kissed me. My heart.

Listening to Run The Jewels as we wound back down, each song more intense than the last, the snow hitting the windscreen like we were in hyper-speed. Then no more snow. If it wasn't for the remnants on the windscreen, nobody would have believed us. Then only the darkness. Then the lights of a small town and the romance of a diner. Then drinking iced water out of frosted glasses and our long conversation keeping on like we are paddling down a river.

I should say now that you never actually kissed me. I just couldn't resist imagining.

I had come to follow you around for a week or two, to take a little holiday from my life, where we could play at being close. I have this special place carved out for you. I don't know what it is with you. We have always talked like you and I have known each other for decades. It feels like the closest I can get to having something fated; I can almost believe we would always find each other and keep finding each other.

We spent the first week staying up late and talking, talking, talking.

Sometimes I worry that I only really know myself with you, or when I'm meeting someone new. Flirting with them and sitting up with them all night. I can only see myself reflected back in that moment. The way I would like to be. Sometimes I feel flashes of it, perhaps when I am cycling home at night. Gliding down a hill, singing. Then I can feel that same confidence again. I feel like I could possibly still, at this late stage of the game, be any kind of hero in any kind of story. But mostly it's when someone desires me.

I told you that I felt like I was only the best of myself when I'm with you. You laughed and said, 'I don't think I've ever been the best of myself with anyone!'

Sometimes when we are together I think, 'Aren't we clever that we can do this, mock all these idiots and tell each other everything? Flirt with the line and be safe from it all catching up with us emotionally? Aren't we clever that we won't get hurt by this?'

But who am I kidding? The rest of the time I am haunted by how little you give away. It's the not knowing that I can't stand and I can't get enough of. Inscrutable boys, ever since I was a kid.

On our last night together we were in a resort town, strolling along the main street after dinner and enjoying that for once we were both tourists. Usually, we would be in your city and you would be giving me the guided tour of some new corner, but here I could tell myself that nobody had the upper hand.

The last bar we passed had music playing, and at first we felt shy to go in. A woman in a suede waistcoat was playing a Joni Mitchell song on the guitar to a little group of tables. Then we did. Then we sat down and, realising it was an open mic, turned to each other, thrilled. Shared a little gleeful look that meant we could be rude about it and in love with it all at once. Then I was at the bar as you walked onstage.

I don't know whose guitar you borrowed. I didn't know you could sing like that. I didn't even know you could play.

And the romance of that song. Light in my head. You in my arms.

And the whole time I tried to work it out. Is he playing this song for me? Is he singing this song to me? My heart in my mouth. I couldn't work you out, and I wasn't even sure I wanted to. Is he playing this song for me? Did he write this song for me? Is that why he has brought me here?

When you sat down again and I handed you a bottle of beer, I kissed you on the cheek. I told myself tonight was the night we would begin. That you had written it for me and the wait had been agony for you too.

But nothing happened. Not when I reached out and pressed my hand to your chest on the train, when it felt like something else was controlling it, something supernatural. Not when we shared a bed. Not when I tried. I ached for you to.

On the flight home was when I realised the song was a cover. The Waterboys. 'Fisherman's Blues'. A band my mum would play on tapes in the car after Dad left. Why it had felt so deep and familiar. It hurt.

And I told myself it was probably for the best. I went out with a songwriter once. He sent me rough recordings, and I told myself that he was singing to me. I heard songs about his ex and I thought: ha, she couldn't win him round. I thought I could have the glory of him falling for me. I should have known I'd have more in common with her than him. Of course I ended up a bitchy footnote. I took so many screenshots of text messages where he had said he loved me, as if that gave me evidence to counter how he made me feel. What was fucking wrong with me? So desperate. Knowing that the moment when you know it won't work out and you know they aren't in love with you had already passed. Clinging on to something that had already fallen through my fingers.

But that's it. Someone is either in love with you, or they aren't, and you know. And not knowing means no. But I still can't give up this special place I have kept for you.

I found a photo of you and me, dressed up like soldiers at the town's museum. How funny to have an artefact jump out at me after decades. It's in sepia, like it's from an old-timey saloon, but now the digital print is rubbing off. The way it actually ages surprises itself.

To this day I cannot work it out with you. I don't want it to be the fact that you never quite let me have you. It's not that simple. Because you would always let me come so close to you. Like you knew too that the best we could hope for was a near miss. Keep the idea of romance open and nobody gets hurt. The everlasting, beautiful potential of nothing at all.

What does it matter now, so much water under the bridge? Who cares at this late stage of the game? By this point romance is a solitary pursuit for me. I am only romantic when I'm alone, looking back. Romance is too short-lived with another person, anyway. It's a lifetime on your own.

The Patron Saint
of Lost Causes

I don't care if what I am doing, what we are doing, is hopeful.
We need to do it anyway. Even if there's no hope left, and
everything is hopeless, we must do what we can.

— Greta Thunberg

I don't finish my tea. I didn't pick up much to eat. A
couple of the apples, and they're not yet at their best. Lucy
wanted me to try the granola she made, and I had to give
it a swerve. Everything here is diplomacy. Her experiments
put food to waste, but most people grin and bear them.

She gives a lot to other people. It makes her happy, that's a good.

I don't feel like I have woken up. I can't stop rubbing my eyes, and the feeling that I'm still asleep won't go. Breakfast is usually my favourite time of the day. I like to come down early and see everyone drift in and out. See the service crank into life, spend time around the children, like a sunrise in themselves. I like reading old papers and filling in the crosswords. And I have never got bored of real baked bread, real churned butter. Milk from the dairy and the thick crust of cream on the rim of the jug.

I scrub my mug and leave it to drain. It sits and waits for the others to come down. I don't. I open the glass doors and walk out across the lawn. Misty and dewy and fresh and as cool as the day will get. I have about an hour until I start work, so I walk to the edge of our fields, to the old bank of the river.

When we first moved in we would swim there. It was just about deep enough to dive in, but never so deep that you couldn't bob down to the bottom. It was cold in the winter, but in a bracing way that made us squeal and scream, giggle and shout out, 'I'm alive, I'm here!' And other similar nonsense. The kids would spend most of the summer falling off rope swings. The toddlers would run in and out of the shallow water, little feral naked things. At first the adults would supervise them, but we had too much to do back at the house, so we left them to it. It took me weeks to accept that they were safe. I was used to following the kids round the park, hands held underneath them while they took on the easy climbs of the equipment. The adjustment was out of my hands; there was simply too much to do. So many repairs, and then so much to build and make.

I let my feet dangle off the bank and my mind go wherever it wants. I remember decamping down here after work and everyone eating outside. Before we were up and running, when we could buy plastic packets of hamburger buns and ready-made veggie burgers. Punnets of strawberries from the larger farm down the road. Bottles of wine and letting the kids stay out running wild. Carrying Thomas back on my shoulders, Dan holding Rosa by the hand while she chatted away. Long grass and blackberries, walking through the dark and listening out for bats' tiny clicks, waiting to see them flit past. My memories mix the years up together, but I like them more for it.

I spit out the last of my sour little apple, and it rolls down into the dust. There's a trickle of water still, but it's dark and not enough to paddle in. I really used to bathe so often. Quick showers and endless baths. It was leisure for me. I liked making a bath so hot that it was a challenge to lower my body into it. Like being scratched all over. Plastic bottles of bubble bath, shower gel, shampoo. The forbidden pleasure of running a shower head into my ear or against my body to masturbate. Minutes and hours of the hot water. I miss it, but I miss the river the most.

It was alive and now it's dead. I was young and suddenly here I am.

I can't spend today dwelling on what I cannot change. Grant me the serenity, grant me the wisdom. Whatever the prayer is, I will say it.

I get to the polytunnels as the day is getting hotter and the wind is starting up. We have managed to shift a lot into hydroponics, but we still try to keep what we can of the original farm. Endless bloody meetings about it, as if we still have any control over planning anything. I think that's what's kept us together at least. No time or energy for enmity when we get enough of that from outside.

I jump out of my skin as I hear him come in behind me, and he laughs his gentle laugh at me.

'It's only me, isn't it!'

'Yes, alright. I didn't know who was on shift with me.'

I knew perfectly well he was on shift with me when I signed up to be on shift with him. He raises one eyebrow and smirks at me, and we laugh together as we start work. We are used to each other, worn in and comfortable, and I like my days with him.

The first few years were so busy. It didn't help that half of us had toddlers and babies and the other half were trying to make them. I never rested. But I also felt everything around me starting to calm down. My body itself was thanking me. The feeling you can get when all you see is greens and browns and the only concrete colour is the clouds. I didn't even realise I had been so stressed, and angry, and aggrieved, until I could feel the absence of it. It was a novelty to wake up, and to feel fine.

When I first left university I moved into a big house

in Denmark Hill with my friends. We threw parties and sat up late with each other. Someone was always feeling sociable, and I was content. We used to joke that, in your first year there, London wanted to kill you. And then after a few years it decided to let you live. Not out of any affection, mind, but more out of boredom. Like a lion bored of swatting a mouse with its giant paws. I had ambitions to live in a house in the inner suburbs. A house! But back then it seemed possible, reasonable even. And then I was thirty-five, and I sat on buses and trains and tubes trying to manage my simmering resentment. I hadn't realised that London was trying to kill me again. The air pollution was making my mind feel sick. It was already so much hotter each summer that I couldn't think straight. I started fantasising about murdering my landlord, about blowing up the Shard and the Cheese Grater, or simply smashing in every single estate agent's window, then moving on to their faces. On the bus, trying and failing to breathe down the rage if I skimmed through a tabloid. The complete and total rage at the monsters in power and the wankers who chose them. Normal stuff, but there was no peace. Living in ground-floor flats that felt like basements, made from converted garages. Years and years in immiserating little holes, where as soon as you walked in, the ceiling hit you in the eyes, stamping you down. I couldn't give up the twenty-year-old I had been who had moved there. I couldn't give up the ghost of how I had hoped things would be, and I kept going like a zombie.

The farm used to be a monastery, and it was a miracle that we made it up here. Seven of us in the first group, with as many kids on top of that. Our flimsy little coalition of savings, our desperate attempts at a split mortgage. We spent two years being outbid by developers and rental companies. And then, we simply weren't. We found somewhere too remote and too run-down for them. And we came here, and I joked it was a pilgrimage. Above the main door is a statue, and I relished teaching the children that it was Saint Christopher, patron saint of travellers. None of us are Christians, but I have always loved the saints. I used to imagine him guiding us here. I used to think of this place as an ark, that the whole world could flood and we would be safe.

Jem is standing right in front of me. 'You alright today?'

'Oh, you know.'

'Oh yes, I know.'

We get back on with the day, checking in on as much of our crops as we can, trying to keep them alive and to work out when and what we can harvest. Chatting and not chatting, standing close to one another. It comforts me.

Until last week I had forgotten that we used to flirt. So hard. And that for a full couple of years I nursed the deepest crush on him, the absolute pain it used to cause me. Rosa was nine and Thomas was seven. Jem and Sara had just moved their family to the new wing of the house. That year we went from twenty to forty people. It was chaos. It was wonderful. I didn't realise what I had missed. There were so many new people around to navigate and test the waters with. So much conversation and argument. I didn't realise that part of me had been hibernating until she was wide awake and making me feel alive again.

He made me laugh, and I was powerless to it. His eyes were always telling me something in private. The promise of mischief. He had been a joiner in Glasgow before they moved here, and I was fixated on his weathered hands. The strength that he carried about with him with such levity. I started plaiting my hair and wearing lipstick. I had forgotten the pass I made at him and how gracious he was in dodging it. How Dan didn't seem to notice the whole thing come and go. Then last week I was walking down the main stairs and the memory hit me like I had bumped into it. I had to stop and grip the banister as my whole nervous system was flooding and I felt bright red all over. Still mortifying after all these years. It took until the bottom of the staircase to let it go. What does it matter now? I looked up at stained-glass Jesus behind me on the landing and let the light cover me. Not technically Jesus anymore. One of the children lovingly repainted him as some kind of rainbow lizard. It makes the whole place clash with greens and blues and purples. Some days it feels stupid and some days it feels dazzling.

Dan used to have an earnestness to him that was very powerful. He could draw people into anything. It's how we got here at all, I'm certain of it. We were both teachers at a secondary academy in Bow, but the kids actually liked him. When they found out we were together his form almost tried to intervene, they were so disgusted. Like the audible shock when I told a class I was thirty-four, that had them all flinching and scrambling to reassure me that I didn't look that old, that I couldn't possibly be so ancient. When we got together I kept trying to find the cynicism in him, to wheedle it out of him. He always had a project, he always had people to organise and his chat was always about hope. Relentless, resetting hope. The man would fall asleep on the night of the apocalypse and wake up hopeful the next morning. There was a songwriter back then that I loved. Her music was doomed and romantic, and a line from one of her songs washes around my head now when I think of him giving a speech, or spending all our weekend rallying folk at a protest, trying and failing to stop a bailiff, or playing folk music to bored teenagers: 'And I sometimes find you childish, and I sometimes find you mesmerising.'

I never liked popular music. I never really liked anything popular. I suppose I'm an awkward soul. My grandmother drummed into me as a child that I wasn't to pay attention to what everyone else was doing, and I took it to heart. It wasn't that I didn't try to fit in. I just loved what I loved, and I kept thinking one day it should be popular too. I didn't think our politics were niche, but the papers screamed it at me. Drunk uncles at weddings shouted it at me. Where Dan's commitment seemed to send people incandescent with fury, it made me like him more. People hated that his life showed them up, and I was proud of him. Proud of our obscure tastes and eccentricities. Only, now, it feels so lonely. I try to remember more than that one line of the song. I can't find it; it just swims and swims round in a circle, and there is nobody here to remember it with me.

When we take a break for lunch we hurry through the wind, scarves over our mouths, and the high door to the kitchen slams behind us. Carrot soup, lentil bread, butter and cheese, fruit tea. All good, all fresh. We say our usual gratitudes to one another, to the farm, to this place. That we are lucky is our whole world. We are lucky to be so far north where nobody cares to bother us. We are lucky to have the farm. We are lucky to have each other. We are lucky the motorway flooded and cut us off. We are lucky, and I believe it, but it doesn't sit well with me. Once I saw a news video about a volcanic explosion on La Palma in the Canary Islands. Footage from a drone showed one little cottage, its lawn and garden bordered by a neat line of trees, sitting pretty, as on each side of the stone fence, rivers of lava, glowing and steaming, flowed down. Sparing this tiny new island as they took the entirety of the last one. We are lucky in the way that that house is lucky. A little cosmic joke.

'Do you remember this song from – God knows – twenty . . . twenty-five years ago?'

I try to sing it to Jem.

He laughs. 'Not really my scene. Sing it again.'

Lucy comes to listen and doesn't know it either. That's no surprise. Before long it becomes a game. You can always trust Jem to start one, and children are singing 'Twinkle, Twinkle, Little Star' for me. It's warm. It's good. I let it go. I come back to where I am.

Part of moving here for me was setting up the school. Being in charge of the children. Dan and I had made grand plans. History and politics and literature. People's history and radical politics and revolutionary literature, of course. And music and art and drama and dance and all the subjects they stopped teaching – the subjects the rich kept only for their own rich children.

I had two little dreams for our utopia: I wanted to pass on my love of the people who our children were named after. To pass on the politics that felt like our religion. Let the children paint pictures of Thomas Sankara and John Maclean and Rosa Luxemburg and understand who they were named after. I wanted to pass on how I had felt reading about them, like I had a home in the world. When we chose the school room I painted 'Another World Is Possible' above the wainscoting, bold and bright red around the room. To live like we were in the early days of a better world, as we used to say when I was a young woman. Always focusing on the starts of their lives and not the ends.

I had also been spending my time online looking at old books from the Middle Ages. The Book of Days, the Labours of the Months. The rhythms people lived their lives in time to. I fantasised about the monks and their rigid days and weeks, and I nurtured the fantasy of study and honest toil to myself. I wanted to strip back everything and connect with the land we now had to look after. To keep the kids in the swing of the seasons and the right things to do with each month and at each time of the year. Equinoxes, solstices, all those things I had never myself been aware of.

Maybe it was more for me, but I wanted them to have deep roots here. And I felt that we could have as many feast days and festivals as medieval peasants but with enough of the modern world to shelter us. It felt beautiful. I was a romantic back then.

When we got here I became a connoisseur of the rain. Hazy or light or sheets, I felt like I was learning the hundred words for snow. I remember the gloomy solicitor who helped us get here promising us no more than seven good days each year. But even he couldn't believe the lucky runs of fair weather we got those first few summers. Lucky. Lucky like running 'into the fire, into the flood, into the hurricane'. Another line from another song I loved and can't remember.

And once things started to change they sped up, and then came the relentlessness of it. Battered by storms, never feeling like we could get a firm footing. Trying to teach the children got harder. I was used to teenagers but I wasn't prepared for my own teenagers. I wasn't ready for them at all: bright, wild, powerful creatures who were devoted to outsmarting me. I wasn't ready for the world that would be around us. I was prepared for one which was long gone.

I used to love slogans on banners at protests. They had good jokes. People thought we were humourless, but it was quite the opposite. We laughed and chanted and sang back then, even as we were charged by police horses. It was a badge of honour for us that we took the piss out of them. And at home on our phones it was quotes, cartoons and memes, sent round to make us all feel together and certain.

I wanted that kind atmosphere for our wee school. We sewed our own banners. There was a saying I loved: 'They tried to bury us. They didn't realise we were seeds.'

But what did I know about planting seeds? I had lived my whole life in London. I saw it all as one event, one gesture. One single solution to our lives as they were, to our worries about everything. You don't just plant a seed and walk away from it. A seed doesn't simply give you a plant. I didn't think about how we would tend to them. I didn't think about germinating and planting the same seeds, nursing and replanting the same plants every single fucking year. That you can tend to a seed all you like, but when the ground is frozen and the water is poisoned it doesn't matter what it is you're planting.

You could grow crops in a heat and a drought that meant fruit didn't wither on the vine, it boiled. Our children, budding in a time when the world was too hot for them to flower. Or maybe it was my generation who couldn't cope with it. Nothing coming at the times it should, with nothing making sense anymore.

I felt something coming a while before the others did because I saw it in the school room every day. And don't get me wrong, it was a lovely time too. We had festivals and dressing-up and ceilidhs and May Day parades and home brew, and we persuaded folk to come from the town so we could have concerts with more interesting music and pot lucks with different dinners. But even so, people could feel it brewing, even without as much contact with the rest of the country.

We were never meant to be a closed community. We always meant for this place to be a harbour for people. It was Dan's big plan. To get people to come and organise. To allow people to come and do so in secret, where it was necessary. There used to always be guests back then. People we knew from all kinds of networks that we helped keep in place. Students too. Always carefully vetted, mainly to keep out devil's advocates and overgrown school debaters. You could always find some group of interesting-looking folk sitting up in the kitchen. I loved them for bringing up bottles of red wine and talking so animatedly, keeping us all updated and in good spirits. It was harder once the options to get online got fewer. Harder still, later on. It was all so unreliable.

It's hardest to put it all together in my memory. I remember the days but not the weeks they came from. I look back at my old diaries, and they are nothing but my emotions. They just seem trivial now. I didn't write about what was happening out in the world, or about how I felt about it. Maybe it seemed too obvious to write down. As if I could ever forget the chaos and the grief. Maybe it's because we were talking and having so many meetings about it. All the adults sat in the dining hall, agreeing and shouting. The fear. All of us mostly on the same page but feeling lost over what could be done. I tried to focus on what I could build, what I could control. It was always less than I hoped.

'Our babies are doing well! Better than last year even! Got a good summer up here at least.'

We are up in what used to be a guest dormitory tending

to the hydroponics: tomatoes, peppers, leaves, weed, herbs. It's so vast and so alive it easily spends the afternoon for us. It's precious and wonderful. Kept alive always by solar panels which will last until I am gone. And then God knows. The eerie futuristic light up here. The greenhouse smell. It's a good job to have, and we can't help but be proud of ourselves. My little project with him.

I want to be satisfied, but my mind dwells on the meetings before they left. All the while I try to work, to make conversation and to harvest the tomatoes I remember the meetings. I try, but I can't remember the night that the decision was made. I see Dan in the great hall, looking more and more like an evangelist and mostly driving me crazy. I remember him: wide-eyed, long hair like a lion's mane, his beard rewilding his face. Clenching his fists and squaring up to some of the others – to his friends of twenty years. Barely suppressing a fight.

He and Sara stood shouting at each other over the rows of plastic chairs. She was from Yorkshire, with long grey hair parted down the middle. She was five foot and made from strips of sinewy muscle, like a rock climber. I had never really seen her angry, and she was formidable. She picked up a chair but didn't want to throw it. Jem managed to joke about it. During it. Trying to puncture the atmosphere with a little mischief, but nothing would deflate it. Nothing would make it go away. My son then standing up, all of fifteen, giving his first speech, in the style of his father. A boy built to sway people.

The clearest memory I have is the night they finally went. A flimsy little brigade. I can't shake the sight of how committed

Thomas and Rosa were, feeling that they had somewhere now to pour out the fighting spirit we had drummed into them. Dan still trying to convince me that they were not in any danger, that they would all be back soon, and me feeling for the first time what a hollow trick he was pulling in believing that. One person leading half our little household in a few vans. What could they possibly do that would be worth the risk? And me crying and not being able to stop. Begging them to stay with me. Watching them leave and watching the lights of the convoy disappear over the brow of the hill one by one. Standing outside until I was soaked utterly.

For a long time after they went I felt I was holding my breath. I would catch myself in a state of tension and not be able to relax myself. I waited for post that never came, for arranged visitors who simply didn't arrive. News seeped in gradually like wet rot. We focused on keeping ourselves safe. Repairing the roof, sustaining the farm, keeping ourselves as self-sufficient as we could. Some folk moved in from the village, and we tried to accommodate them and not to ask questions.

The rest of that year was agony. I felt like I was rotting. I felt like we were in permanent darkness and it was fitting. My children's lives were one short winter's day: why shouldn't the rest of mine be?

It was sometime during that season, which must have lasted a couple of years, that I was trying to salvage what I could from the old library after a flood. We had left the gutters above it too long between clearing them, and a minor storm punished us for it. We lost a lot of books, but most of them had been inherited from the monks anyway. All of the library I'd brought and cultivated had survived, and I felt painfully glad of it. As I lifted the sodden ancient lumps onto a trolley I found a little reference pamphlet for visitors to the place, from back when the monastery took in people on retreats and pilgrimages. It had the energy of the last century, not even an inkling that things might change. I sat and looked through my home before it was mine, finding out who had painted some of the old portraits, who had set the stained glass and designed the building's layout. And on the last page there was my Saint Christopher, except it turns out he never was. He was Saint Jude, the patron saint of lost causes.

It shifted here away from hope. Since they left. Since they didn't come back. It shifted to gratitude. It shifted to any straws we could collectively grasp. The work stops you getting depressed, but it doesn't stop you despairing. It was hard to feel like we had been right and it had made no difference. We were right that leaving wouldn't end well, and yet I think of Dan with his invincible heart and I can't fault him. I don't know. We were all so earnest. We tried very hard. Some of us tried one way and some of us tried another, and some days I see us as saints and other days as idiots. For all its disappointments, we tried. Soon it will be someone else's turn.

'Will we call it a night?' he says to me.

How does he still manage a twinkle in his eye? He started out as one type of man and he just stuck to it. Even after

Sara died. He was lucky to have her as long as he did. I never would have dreamed that my return to the Middle Ages would be through a lack of medicine. Hydroponics and solar panels and dying for want of antibiotics.

'Lucy playing her guitar for folk, is that tonight?'

'Aye, she'll be playing her full repertoire. Three songs by Ed Sheeran and half of "Streets Of London".'

We laugh and grimace and pretend we are too good for the easy company. These days I take whatever I can get. If it's seven good days a year, I treasure them. When my children were young I lived in a permanent feast of good days, and I was so well fed I didn't think to save them up.

'Well, how can you tell me you're lonely?' I say. Oh, I can remember every word of that pile of shite.

'Exactly. I might take a rest beforehand. Gather my strength for the onslaught.'

'I'll see you at dinner.'

'You will.'

I go into the deconsecrated chapel and I pray to St Jude for all of us. I pray the lines I remember from an old folk song: 'There's a better world, and on a quiet day, when I hold my breath I can hear her say she's on her way. Take heart. Take heart. Take heart.'

The songs here (sometimes misquoted but all reproduced with kind permission) are 'Natural Successor' by Pictish Trail, 'I Can't Keep You' by Ex:Re and 'The Losing Side' by Grace Petrie.

I Don't Know

My partner is away, and I am lying in between my children. My three-year-old is pushing me to the edge of our big bed, kneeing me in the back in her sleep. My three-month-old is in a tiny cot next to the bed. She wakes up to feed, and I try not to turn on the night light as I lift her up to lie down next to me. Please God, don't let this wake her sister. It's no use. My older daughter wakes up and thinks it is the morning. 'Why do we need trees?' at full volume is her opener for the day. I am so hopelessly tired. Last night I begged her to go back to sleep and started to cry. Then I lay there, feeling so sick with guilt that I had lost it with her that I couldn't get back to sleep myself.

It's dumb to say, but I love my daughter so much. Sometimes I am so struck by her little face. My mind bends staring at her. I cannot believe she is mine. I cannot believe how beautiful she is. I cannot believe that I recognise her, and then I don't recognise her, and then I have been staring too long and it's like repeating a word till it's just the sounds. I sing her a song every night that goes: 'I love you every day! I love you every day! I love you on a Monday, Tuesday, Wednesday, Thursday, Friday, Saturday, Sunday. I love you every day! No matter what you say! I love you when you're happy, grumpy, silly, sad or stinky.' I finally feel like someone has the best of me when I love her as much as I do.

I love the baby too, but it is a different, more primal thing with a baby. I sit with my little baby as she wraps her tiny fingers around mine. I stare into her little eyes, her dear little face. She breaks off the breast to smile at me. This dear little thing who has never hurt anyone, who I still believe never could. I feel like my heart is wide open to the whole world. I watch a video of a mother and son tap dancing and pause it so that I can burst into tears, thinking: how can anyone be cruel? I feel vulnerable and tender all the time. I only see the good in everyone I meet. I want to mother every human, every animal, every plant even, that I see.

I am a sweet sad cow with a mind that won't stop racing. And this is how I am, while I lie awake unable to get back to sleep. I cannot stop thinking that we have left the Holocene.

I Don't Know

I think of how things were when I was a child, I think of my grandpa's house. Palm Sunday fronds from church and Easter Day mini-gardens. Slow worms slinking away as we turned over stones in the flower beds. The little playhouse he made us, the sweet smell of mildew and a drawer full of biscuits. I think of his garden, cluttered with life, the seasons flowing, so easygoing. I think of myself sat safely in the 1980s, five years old, in the garden playing with a box of tin soldiers they had kept for us. Little tin Americans fighting little tin Germans. I was closer then to the Second World War than I was to now, but it could have been a hundred years before, to my mind.

The only time the weather acted out of turn was one freak hurricane. It caused such a big stir that we talked about it for decades. Whether or not it woke us up in our little cabin beds and bunk beds. My father taking us to the local woods to inspect the damage. Taking stunned photos on a film camera. I say it was a different world, but it was a different world.

I know this is ridiculous, but sometimes it makes no sense to me that I can't revisit it. How can the past be the only place you can't travel back to? I can't visit six or seven again, not once? And how can it be that this journey is only one-way, that I will just keep getting older? To fifty, then sixty, seventy if I am lucky, but never just back to thirty-five for a bit, coasting back and forth from thirty to thirty-five, feeling my lovely squishy joints and light energetic mind. All this cannot be real. It doesn't seem fair.

I'm stupid to say it felt safe back then though. It was the same time that I was certain I was going to die in a nuclear war. When my mother, as a joke, taught me to say 'inter-continental ballistic missile'. But I suppose it didn't feel as certain as it does right now. I sing songs to the baby while I read about fire season on my phone. I look at maps of the world where half of it is dark red. I see the government react with barbarism and I try to protest. Every news article is the start of a disaster movie, but it just keeps on coming. And with all of that I thought it was a great idea to bring them both into the world. I was evangelical about it even. 'We have to face it all with optimism,' I would say. And it's not even like I've changed my mind, so much as you can't ever know what you're getting into before it arrives.

I remember that before I had my big daughter – 'big', all of three, so silly, but here we are – you couldn't have told me what it was like not to sleep, for years on end, to adjust gradually, slapped by moments of genuine horror, to the fact that I would always be a parent, always care so deeply about her that it could scare the shit out of me. I could have told you that I understood but I could never really have *known* it.

'Why are bums private?' she says, and I am weighing up what and how to tell her. What I am right or wrong to introduce. I do this kind of freeform hedging when I can't yet work out how to explain things. 'Well, of course, darling, um, well, they are private because they are a private place that belongs to only you, and nobody should touch them except you.' 'But why?' Totally fair follow-up – I'm not answering, I'm a real politician on this one.

I try to distract her while I feed the baby. Not even 7 a.m. Not the day yet as far as I am concerned, but unable to enforce. I used to grieve the lack of sleep, but now I try to find clever games to cheat it even for a second. My partner invented 'hide-and-seek toys', where he makes her shut her eyes and then throws her toys around the room, desperately hoovering up little crumbs of sleep as she goes to retrieve them. It doesn't work for me as she is never quiet. All the traits I admire – being loud, being outspoken, being ingenious, being rebellious – they are all a fucking nightmare to parent. I am hoping this second one will stay a sleepy little potato.

'Can you go to the bathroom and put your night nappy into the bin, please?'

'It's not a nappy.'

'Oh yes, of course it isn't. My mistake, it's a big girl's dry nights pants.' Significantly different, as we have arbitrated over several difficult weeks. Woe betide the two-year-olds we know with their babyish nappies. She has moved on, she likes to explain.

'Okay, darling?'

She is considering her next move, and I am holding my breath, desperate she won't think of something to make things more difficult.

'Okay, Mummy.'

And off she trots like a little baby goat tip-tapping into the bathroom.

There is a minute of soft, sweet, warm and beautiful sleep before I hear her cry out.

I can breathe in and say 'oh fuck' at the same time, it turns out. I leap out of the bed so quickly it wakes and scares the baby, who starts to scream in a frightened way I haven't heard before.

When I get to the bathroom I don't see anything strange beyond the fact that she is not happy.

'What?! What is it, darling?' And as the ringing in my ears subsides and my cheeks cool down a little bit, I can retain my composure and my playful mum tone of voice. 'What is it, darling? . . . Oh, darling, don't worry. Mummy was just shouting because she was scared. Don't worry, it's okay. Now, what's going on?'

She doesn't say anything but she points down to the nappy bin, which is somewhat full.

'What, darling?'

And then I notice that it seems to be full of a kind of flowing, dark liquid. And then I notice that the flowing, dark liquid is actually on the floor too. All over the floor. And the bath mat. And her clothes from last night's bath that I hadn't yet had the energy to clear up. The liquid is everywhere and it is moving, and it is not liquid at all, but it is a sea, alive with little maggot-like worm things. And she has one in her hand. And the baby is still screaming, and I feel nauseous and like I need an adult, but of course the adult is me. It's not fair!

'Stay where you are, don't move, put it down. I mean, put it back. Put it back!' I bark, but trying still to bark in a fun way. I run to grab the baby, and my foot squashes something on the hall carpet, and I see it is also alive. Messy and teeming with life.

I remember when I was in labour with the little one. She was back to back, and it was excruciating. Such a shock, such a surprise for it to be so different to my first, calm birth. As if the way the planet had changed in the three years between them had meant that she was angry in advance about what I was bringing her into. It was so painful that I couldn't bear to labour alone. First time, I used a TENS machine for days, gently breathing, gently everything. This time, I was screaming and crying out. Swearing to amuse myself so that laughing could somehow soften it. And in all that chaos, it was at 6 a.m., as my partner rang the hospital, that my big girl padded into the room. Curious more than frightened, as she always is. I decided that screaming would scare her, so I tried to tell her a line from a book we had read together.

'It's the baby's birthday today,' a voice said from my mouth. 'It's the baby's . . . aaagh . . . moooooooooo!'

In the grips of roaring agony I improvised a moo. I thought that might make it fun. It didn't not work. But it wasn't a roaring success either.

And back in the bathroom, with the baby disorientated and blinking her little tears away, I tried to think of how to moo this one.

Creepy crawlies. I don't think I can control how my body feels about them. I start to itch and I start to feel like I will be sick, and they are everywhere. I want to say that it's an instinctive and visceral response, but I look at my daughter and the delicacy she has for them and that can't be true.

I'm reminded of our little walks together during the lockdowns. Me trying somehow to get exercise at a toddler's pace. The dusty dead grass giving way to the sticky tarmac paths of the local park, the swings locked away. She was so thrilled with any creature we encountered. Slow and ponderous with each scrap of moss, each rogue dandelion bursting out between paving stones. I have always tried to teach her to love every living thing. No, no, darling, we don't squash the ant because it's just living its life. No, no, darling, we don't rip the leaves off the hedge because it's just living its life. No, no, darling, we don't pinch hard the faces of the local babies because Mummy needs the mum friends she has just about solidified, for the love of God!

We discussed which flowers we could get away with picking, what would and wouldn't hurt, and I hoped she wouldn't realise my logic was net curtain. We stopped for what felt like, but legally could not have been, hours as she cooed over a spider – 'Hello, Mrs Spider! It's so cute' – in her high, tiny little voice.

I signed her up to an outdoor kindergarten, and it only made her more hardy. Chewing on pigeon feathers before I could work out an explanation as to why it wasn't a good idea. Little bitten nails with caked-in dirt. The things she loves and appreciates that seem ugly or unimportant to me. Like ghosts that only she can see.

She is down on her knees now, her face right up close to a collection of them. Curious and delighted. I try to pick her up and move her with the arm that doesn't have a baby attached. I manage to get her into the bath. Neither of us are happy about it.

'Okay . . . okay . . . right!' I keep saying, like I'm starting a breezy new slate each time. A short-circuiting robot with a manic smile. I find my phone and google them, and I learn in that moment that there's an indoor kind of beetle and that it's big and I have several thousand of them.

I realise that I have to kill them.

I don't even think that I can.

I don't kill anything except mosquitos, because fuck mosquitos. I've had too many bites not to kill mosquitos. I never encountered one as a child and now they are everywhere and I feel no guilt whatsoever when I squish one. I am not a killer. Except, I guess, I eat meat. But I feel terrible about it. And I dread the day she realises properly that we eat animals. I've seen a video of a little boy, realising that what he is eating was a real–life octopus, descending into sobs of pure compassion, his mother saying (in Spanish, but with subtitles), 'My darling, we don't have to eat them anymore.' I keep expecting it from my daughter, but it hasn't come. I'm clinging to her ignorance until I have to change.

'Okay . . . okay . . . right!'

Long story short, I tell her that they love to swim, and she helps me flush every single one of them down the toilet.

I make it fun.

I make her smilingly complicit. I told her they love swimming, and that for a treat we are taking them swimming. The baby gurgles joyfully on a bouncer.

Is that better? Is that worse? The more we pick up, the more I see the beauty and character in them. Little grey furry grubs, reaching out and clawing blindly as they stretch their pairs and pairs of legs. The more we pick up, the more fun she is having and the worse I feel.

'There you go! Go swimming with your mummy and daddy' in her dear little voice. Her precious little voice that has had so many iterations already. Each one is so fleeting. I get used to a sweet mispronunciation – 'aminal' for animal, 'nursiye' for nursery – and then it's gone, and she can say it right, and I'm gutted about it. I tried some of the times to use the baby word myself, to see if I could get one more time of hearing her say it, but she would blank me entirely. That version of her was long gone. Too fast, unfair. How can it be possible even that her baby self is gone, her year-old self is gone, her two-year-old self is gone. And it is going to be this forever. Only knowing what is lost once I've lost it.

Is it better or worse to tell her? I don't know. There is so much that I am trying to hold at bay, to keep at arm's length. Just for a small time more. Just for one more little iteration of her.

There are so many things I hide from myself on a daily basis to keep up my charade of just living my life. We are well fed while other people are starving. We are safe while other people flee danger. There are so many things I fail to block out that I know I should be spending every second of every day fighting against, yet I don't.

That night I lie awake and I feel so guilty for what we did, and I feel grief for the world I wanted them to have, the one that I didn't manage in time to make. Deaths I cannot prevent. The life for them I cannot create. I have to keep faith, but all I can think of is that the people in power who I fought and couldn't stop being elected have less compassion for human beings than my child has for animals, for insects, for leaves.

I want to think my children will be brave and resilient. People want to keep saying how we are all so much stronger than we know, so much more resilient than we realise. No. It's the opposite. We are all so much more fragile than we realise. We can't unsee anything. It takes so little to completely break us and throw us off course. If we knew how little we could actually bear, we would be so much gentler with each other, with the world.

When both of them were born it was this wonderful, instant glowing feeling, almost just out of relief that they were here. And when both of them were born I said the same thing to them, the first thing they ever heard on this earth: 'Hello, darling!' Because when I was a child, my mother would always say to me, 'The first thing I ever said to you, the first words you ever heard on this earth, were "hello, darling".' And I used to walk around school thinking that I was somebody pretty special indeed. And so when I had mine, I kept enough presence of mind to pass that on. 'Hello, darling!' I wept as they were placed like little scrabbly aliens onto my chest. 'Hello, darling, I love you.'

How can I bring someone into this world when it feels like apocalypse is everywhere. What kind of world am I bringing them into? At least for now it can be my world. Where my house is your whole world, and it is safe and it is beautiful and it can be fun.

I am not bringing you into the world. I am bringing you into my world. The rules do not apply.

I do not think everything will be alright, but when I am lying in between them I can convince myself that enough will be. Enough will be alright to keep going. And what's with 'alright' anyway? How drab. Enough will be wonderful. Hello, darling, welcome to the world! Enough – enough will be wonderful!

Acknowledgements

First, thank you so much to Grace Petrie, Johnny Lynch and Elena Tonra for the generous permission to reprint their lyrics in 'The Patron Saint Of Lost Causes'.

So many people have been so kind to me in helping me write this book and I want to thank them.

I want to thank my partner Jonny Donahoe for holding Dr baby and entertaining Mrs baby while I wrote this book. We are very lucky to have you and I love you a lot.

Thank you to my mum for supporting me in being creative as a child, for putting me on to stand-up comedy, for indulging me and entering me into poetry competitions, and for telling me I was the best one in school plays when I most certainly wasn't.

Thank you to Jimmy Symonds who taught me how to enjoy writing, and to Dr Sharon Butler who was so encouraging of my writing and kind to me when I didn't have a place to study. Thank you to Ben Hewitt for supporting my writing at university and helping me keep the faith that one day I could do this. Thanks to Nick Taylor and fuel for commissioning my stories in the past, too.

Thank you to Francis Bickmore for taking a comedian seriously as a writer and for being such a cool and laid-back person to work with re: deadlines and ADHD! Thank you to everyone at Canongate for being so kind to me.

Thank you to Gordon Wise and to Bríd Kirby and to Kelly van Valkenburg for being so supportive of me and my work and for being brilliant people to know and work with.

I want to thank the Coodoop aka Nikesh Shukla for being such an incredibly supportive friend and mentor to me, and for giving me the confidence to think that I would be able to do this. I wouldn't have been able to write this without your help.

Thanks forever to Isy Suttie, Bisha K. Ali, Julie Bower, Michael Segalov, Daniel Harkin, Neil Griffiths, Maeve Higgins, Natasha Brett, Douglas King, Robin Ince and Henry Bell for their creative camaraderie and tireless supportive friendship. I don't deserve you but you are stuck with me!

And thank you to my wonderful friends who have read my writing and reassured me that it isn't criminally bad:

Acknowledgements

John-Luke Roberts, Tom Parry, Mark Watson, Nell Frizzell, Phoebe Elkins, Flannery O'Kafka, Phil Chambers, John Robins, Monica Heisey, Liam Williams, Simon Renshaw, Eleanor McDowall, Ella Duncan, Josh Weller and Allisa Murphy McFarlen. I appreciate it very much. Thank you to Joel Golby and Nathalie Olah for reading a story when I enthusiastically foisted one on them, too! I hope I didn't forget anyone.

Thank you to every landlord, misogynist, prick and Tory who inspired the villains. One day we will win and you will lose and it will be very nice indeed.